G000126512

A GRIM HAUNT

Rachel Stanley

Stanley Publications

Copyright © 2021 Rachel Stanley

All rights reserved.

ISBN: 978-1-8380272-3-0

For key workers the world over.

CONTENTS

ACKNOWLEDGEMENTS

If you're wondering why this book is dedicated to key workers the world over, then let me explain. The majority of *A Grim Haunt* was written in 2020 (with editing being finished in 2021). As you'll probably know, during that time the whole world was at risk because of a newly emerged virus. While scientists everywhere worked desperately to develop a vaccine, our key workers ensured that we had food to eat, that lines of communication remained open, and that our health was prioritised. And that's why I've chosen to dedicate this book to key workers the world over, those people who continued to go out and work despite the risks they faced by being out and about. This is my way of expressing my gratitude to them.

Of course, I'm also extremely grateful to my wonderfully supportive family and some fabulous friends: my mum, Margaret Eyre; my brother, Daniel, and his family, Jessica, Ewan, and Esme Eyre; my in-laws, Joan and Peter Stanley; my brother-in-law, Phil Stanley; and one of my best friends, Jessica Cantwell. You all know why you deserve a mention; I won't belabour the point.

You'll notice that I've not yet mentioned hubby. I couldn't do this without his help and support. I can't tell you how often we debate plot points and grammar rules! And I suppose I should also say thank you to Cooper and Watson, my fur babies, for letting me use their names, their looks, and their personalities in both *A Grim Affair* and *A Grim Haunt*. Don't worry, they'll also feature in *A Grim Ending*!

As with *A Grim Affair*, when I thought I was done with *A Grim Haunt*, I sent it to an army of willing volunteers and asked them to savage my work. Version two of *A Grim Haunt* is so much better than version one because they were willing to be honest with me about what they liked and didn't like. Mum, hubby, Jessica Cantwell, Kirsten Flores, Stephen Mills, and Donna White—thank you so much, guys!

There are just a couple more thanks that I need to say. Kate Hargrave and Janan Kelebek helped me with the German, Beck Michaels designed the cover (which I'm sure you'll agree is absolutely stunning), and Donna White and Lee Munro completed the final proofread.

Lastly, I'd like to say thank you to you, my reader. I write because I enjoy writing, because I have characters in my head who want to live a life on paper, but I'd be lying if I said I didn't care what other people think of my work. I love that you want to read what I've written. Hopefully you'll like it, and if you do, please, please, please leave me a review on your preferred platform.

My thanks to you all.

P.S. As with *A Grim Affair*, any mistakes that you find in *A Grim Haunt* are all my own. I may have had help and support, but the final say was always mine, and sometimes I just liked it the way it was. If you find a typo, though, feel free to let me know.

Prologue

Sunday 22nd November 1914

The air was glacial, but there was no escaping it. Its frigid fingers caressed every inch of his body as he huddled further and further into the mud, searching for whatever relief he could find. There was no real comfort to be had there though; the ground was icy cold and damp. The trenches offered nothing more than a hint of safety.

The noise and clamour that had persistently assaulted his senses for so long had finally ceased, so, with a little time to do something other than survive at last, George let his mind wander, grateful for the brief respite. He'd been living a nightmare for the past few days. The fighting had been vicious, and many of his comrades had lost their lives, but from what he could tell, neither side had gained anything. Winter appeared to be the only winner in the battle that had been fought.

George was overwhelmed by the apparent death toll. He knew that if he poked his head above the parapet, he would see hundreds of bodies strewn across no-man's-land. Earlier on in the day occasional groans and cries had echoed through the air, but over time they'd died away and now all was quiet.

As he sat, hunched up in a crevice that he'd dug into the trench wall, shivering from both the cold and his misery, George wondered if the Keeper of Souls was nearby. As he understood it, it was his job to reap the souls of the dying after all.

Prior to being deployed, George had learned all about the Keeper of Souls, his history, and his purpose. He'd been intrigued by the idea of a supernatural being who'd sacrificed his own soul in order to have a child, but it sounded like a fairy tale. So much so that George would have dismissed it as such had it not been his own father who'd relayed the legend to him. His father was too stern to entertain anything that even bordered on the fictional, let alone the fantastical.

George sighed quietly to himself before lifting his hands to his mouth and blowing on them, vainly attempting to warm his fingers through. Frostbite was a very real and present danger. He wiggled his toes for the same reason, idly wondering if the Keeper of Souls was bothered by the freezing weather. He had so many questions. His father had dropped quite the bombshell on him while he'd been packing for the front.

George was relatively bright, he'd had no difficulty comprehending the secrets that had been shared with him, but he remained uncertain about them. To him, brought up against a backdrop of devout stoicism, his father's words had sounded incredulous. How was it possible for anyone to pull their soul out from within their body, let alone use it to create a child? How could that same soul then be passed down through the generations? And perhaps more importantly, to him anyway, why did he have to guard the latest in the line of children? That didn't sound fair. Mind you, George was quickly learning that life was not fair.

George's problem wasn't a conceptual or a theological one. He'd been brought up to believe in God and was well aware that every decision he made would be judged in due course. If he lived a virtuous life, he knew that his own soul would eventually be taken to reside in heaven, where it would sit at the right-hand side of the Almighty. However, if he didn't, it would be doomed to spend all eternity in hell, where it would be feasted upon by the devil himself. If that were the case, though, how could anyone inherit a soul? And putting that issue aside, what he really struggled with, the part of his father's story that he just couldn't quite grasp, was how the Keeper of Souls had impregnated his lover. At sixteen years old, George was fairly certain that he understood where babies came from, but his father had not spoken of any kind of physical interaction. He'd only said that the Keeper of Souls had pushed his soul into his lover's abdomen. Her body had apparently done the rest, but how was that possible? George believed in God, but he didn't believe in magic.

George's ears and cheeks turned pink at the mere thought of sex. A slight flush warmed his body through as the blood surged in his veins. His family was extremely religious, and he'd done nothing more than kiss a girl chastely on the lips before joining the British Army. His thoughts turned to the young woman in question, Mabel. She'd promised to wait for him, and in return, he'd promised to marry her when he got home.

A slight smile ghosted George's face as he thought of his betrothed, not that they'd told anyone of their intent yet. She was petite and slim with chestnut-coloured hair and pale, porcelain-like skin. Her large doe-brown eyes and high cheekbones gave her a look of innocence, which suited her demure and modest demeanour. George had immediately fallen in love with her innate shyness, but he'd soon realised that she hid a quick wit and an agile mind behind those mild manners of hers. They'd spent hours during the summer months lying side-by-side, hand-in-hand looking up at the sky in a meadow near where they both lived, sharing their hopes and dreams with each other. They'd talked about their past and had planned for their future. Mabel wanted lots of children, four at least. She even had names picked out for them, George Junior and Harold for the boys, and Mary and Ruth for the girls. But then he'd had to leave for war, and right before he'd left, his father had laid the weight of destiny upon him.

George had been forbidden to share stories of the Keeper of Souls with anyone else. Only his line—the line of Guardians—knew anything of the Keeper of Souls and what had happened in the past, or so he'd been told. His father had said that if he were the Chosen One, he'd be visited by an angel who would gift him with the relevant powers to do what was necessary. He hadn't been told what the Chosen One was or what action he might need to take though. He hadn't even been told why the children needed guarding.

Despite his misgivings, George was an obedient child. He'd complied with his father's demands not to tell tales and had wrestled with the uncertainty all by himself. Mystical elements aside, his chief dilemma was whether or not he'd be able to fulfil his duties as a Guardian if he had a family of his own.

War was not exactly what George had expected. In his mind it had been a short campaign, almost a vacation. He'd assumed he'd make (and keep) plenty of friends, they'd tussle with the enemy during the day and play games well into the night. George had quickly had his fanciful notions knocked out of him, but he'd retained his sanity by persistently puzzling over what lay ahead of him. He wanted to return from war fit and healthy for his bride.

What George couldn't possibly know was that all of his anxiety was in vain. He was not the Chosen One. While he would indeed spend his life watching over another, he would not be called upon to fight in any other wars. Instead, he would pass on what he'd learned to his youngest, Harold, who would, in turn, pass it on again and so on through the generations until George's great-granddaughter became the Guardian. Her name was foretold and she would be the most important of her line. She was the one that the prophecy spoke of.

Chapter 1 – Emma

Friday 12ᵗʰ April 2019

Blackpool Victoria Hospital, also known as the Vic, was quickly becoming my least favourite place in all the world. While I very much appreciated the medical care and attention that I'd been receiving in recent weeks, I'd had enough. I was fed up with the constant pain, and I wanted to walk without any impediment. And naturally I blamed the building. Well, not really, but I did want to know why the main carpark was located miles away from outpatients. Okay, so not everyone who made the trip down the world's longest corridor (as I'd dubbed the main walkway through the hospital) had been attacked by a crazy nut-bag stalker, picking up any number of cuts and bruises along with a fractured ankle in the process, but it was a really long way to walk for those of us using crutches.

I stopped abruptly, wanting to stretch my hands. It had been roughly eight weeks since my car had been purposely rammed from behind while I'd been driving home late one night. Since then I'd been under strict instructions to keep all of my weight off my ankle, hence the crutches.

My palms felt like they were on fire, so I paused. Unfortunately, because I gave no warning of my intent to those nearby, the person hurrying along behind me had no choice but to butt up against me. A wave of anxiety washed over me; panic threatened to engulf me. It took me a huge degree of effort to crush those feelings and turn to apologise. However, before I could open my mouth and say anything, the strongest sense of deja vu washed over me, and a tiny shiver ran down my spine.

"I'm sorry," I squeaked, finding my voice at last.

"S'okay," a young teenager responded, her voice husky, her distress obvious. She was casually dressed in 'boyfriend' jeans that sat low on her hips, an oversized hoodie that almost drowned her small frame, and a pair of scuffed trainers. She had the hood of her jumper pulled up over her face, so I didn't get a good look at her features, but one word immediately sprang to mind: haunted. It was the only word that I could think of to describe her. Before I could say anything else, she hurried away, leaving me oddly bewildered by the encounter.

"Weird," I mumbled to myself.

"What was that?" Ellie asked, coming up behind me and making me jump. Adrenaline flooded my system once more, causing my stomach to cramp and a bead of sweat to appear on my forehead.

"Don't sneak up on me like that," I snapped, even though Ellie was my very best friend in all the world and had driven me to the hospital for what I was hoping would be my last check-up in a while. She'd even let me out of the car before going off to park in the multi-story, thus saving me at least some of the walk to outpatients.

"I'm sorry," Ellie apologised, a slight smile turning up the corners of her mouth. However, I couldn't help but notice that her eyes didn't sparkle mischievously as they normally would. Worry was etched into her features, but I chose to ignore it. I was fine. I'd repeatedly told everyone I was fine, there was nothing to worry about, nothing to see here.

"I said that was weird," I repeated, despite my irritation, still annoyed at her.

"What was? What happened?" Ellie was either oblivious to the tone of my voice or was simply overlooking it. To be honest, I doubted it was the former.

"That girl," I nodded in the direction that the teenager had headed, my frustration fading away at last, "when she bumped into me, I had the oddest sensation. It was almost as though the exact same thing had happened previously."

"What girl?" Ellie asked, placing a hand on the small of my back and gently coaxing me in the direction of the clinic I was due to attend.

In hindsight, Ellie's question was my first clue that unusual things were beginning to happen again. However, in the moment, I brushed off Ellie's comment, assuming that the teenager was merely lost in the crowd up ahead. Last time I'd seen someone who others couldn't—a tall, dark, handsome stranger—I'd eventually learned that I was soulmates with the aforementioned stranger, also known as Blake, also known as the Grim Reaper, although he had repeatedly told me his correct title was the Keeper of Souls. And I had repeatedly ignored him. Being soulmates with the Grim Reaper sounded so much cooler than being soulmates with the Keeper of Souls. Although I was starting to think that we weren't actually soulmates in the truest sense of the word because that would mean we had matching souls, whereas in actual fact, Blake and I shared a soul between us.

"What girl?" Ellie asked again, intruding on my wayward thoughts.

"She's up ahead; you probably can't see her now. It was the most peculiar sensation when she touched me."

"Peculiar how?"

"I don't really know how to describe it," I answered honestly, a little bit lost for words. "Maybe tingly?" I tried to sum up how I'd felt.

"I thought Blake was the only one who made you feel like that now." Ellie smirked at me, although I could still see the concern in her eyes. "You know, when he takes you in his arms and—"

"Ellie!" I exclaimed, reddening. Although she wasn't wrong. Blake and I did have a lot of . . . erm, well . . . chemistry. I assumed sharing a soul had something to do with that. "You're just jealous," I muttered.

"I sure am," Ellie said, very serious all of a sudden. "I wouldn't kick him out of bed for f—"

"Do you have to?" I interrupted.

"What?" Ellie asked innocently, widening her baby blue eyes as much as she possibly could. "I was only going to say that I wouldn't kick him out of bed for featherbedding."

"Featherbedding? What on earth is that?"

Ellie laughed wickedly. "I've no idea; I just made it up."

"Uh-huh," I responded. Sometimes with Ellie it was wiser to say nothing at all.

"Speaking of Blake," she continued, "how did he take it when you told him he couldn't come with us to the hospital?"

I pulled a face. It wasn't that I didn't want him at the hospital with me, but Blake existed mostly on another plane. The only time he was corporeal was when he was in my 'bubble.' Proximity to me forced him to manifest because essentially I made him whole. He didn't like that wording, of course! However, my sphere of influence was temperamental. Sometimes my radial broadcast was bigger than others, and I hadn't wanted him suddenly disappearing from sight. "Not very well actually. But I need to be able to concentrate on what the doctor's saying; I can't be worrying about him. And anyway, just because I forbade him from coming to my appointment, it doesn't mean he isn't close by. I feel like I can almost sense him."

"He's probably on the roof," Ellie surmised. And she was probably right. One of the things I'd learned about Blake was that he liked to hang out on rooftops. "What do you think the doctor will say then?" she switched subjects seamlessly.

"Well, I hope he says I can get rid of these things," I said, indicating the crutches that I'd absentmindedly strewn next to me when we'd finally gotten to the right waiting area. "After six weeks in a cast and another two being mindful not to put any weight on my ankle, I'm ready to walk again. I'm well and truly sick of this place."

"Don't say that," Ellie chastised, "the staff here have done a brilliant job patching you up. You're just grumpy because of what happened to you."

I exhaled loudly. "I suppose." And I knew she was right. Everyone at the Vic had been wonderful; I couldn't have asked for a better team at my side while on the road to recovery. Mind you, acknowledging that didn't suddenly put me in a better mood. "I think I have a right to be a bit fed up though. The last few months have been pretty rubbish. First of all I was plagued by strange dreams—"

"Which turned out to be of your soulmate," Ellie interrupted.

"And then I thought I was hallucinating because my reflection kept changing," I continued as though Ellie hadn't spoken at all.

"Yes, but that was your ancestors finding a way to connect with you." That was also true. Whenever I caught sight of myself in a mirror now, I often saw one of the people who'd had my soul before me. Mostly it was either the first of my line or my grandmother.

"And lastly I was stalked by a madman who would have killed me if Seith hadn't saved me." Seith was Blake's guardian, as best I could tell anyway. Blake tended to dodge questions about Seith, but I suspected that was because he didn't know all that much himself.

"Well, yes, that last one was a bit on the scary side," Ellie shuddered before continuing, "but Seith did save you, although I suspect Blake would argue it was him rather than Seith who intervened."

"Hmmm, I'm sure he would."

"Come on, your life is awesome." Ellie grinned suddenly. "You're soulmates with the Grim-freaking-Reaper for heaven's sake." And as she said the words 'Grim-freaking-Reaper,' I knew without a doubt that Blake was somewhere close by. A wave of annoyance washed over me that quashed any lingering doubt I might have had. When we were near enough to each other, our emotions would inevitably connect, and Blake hated being called the Grim Reaper.

I told you not to come, I projected my thoughts outwards into the air around me. Another handy facet of being soulmates with the Grim Reaper was that we could talk telepathically, again only when we were near enough to each other though. Blake could read my thoughts as well, but for some reason I couldn't read his . . . yet. I was hoping to acquire that skill eventually.

What, cat got your tongue? I asked when Blake didn't reply. I could have pulled him to me if I'd wanted to do so, but that might have caused a bit of a stir in the windowless waiting room. For some reason, despite the fact that all of our other abilities relied on proximity to each other, no matter how far apart we were, Blake could always hear me calling for him. Although he said that it was more of a tug and that if I really wanted to, I could force him to join me. That irked him somewhat.

"Emma?" Ellie broke into my thoughts. "Your name has been called."

"Oh, has it? Sorry, I was talking to Blake."

"I figured as much."

Sometime later, after being declared 'on the mend' and cleared for gentle weight-bearing activities by Mr. Anish, Ellie and I finally made it back to the main entrance of the Vic. It looked less like a hospital and more like a mini shopping centre complete with coffee shops, food stores, a stationer, and a chemist.

"Coffee?" Ellie asked.

"I suppose," I replied, wondering if I could come up with a legitimate reason not to linger in the hospital.

"You'll be fine, I promise," Ellie reassured, although how she knew what I'd been thinking was beyond me. "Are you going to ask Blake to join us?"

"No."

"He'll be peeved."

"How can he join us without causing a commotion?" I asked. "We'll end up being front-page news: Man Miraculously Appears Out of Nowhere." I brushed aside my inner turmoil and channelled Ellie, doing my best to dramatize the headline.

"You could go into the bathroom and call for him in there."

"And walk out of the ladies with a man in tow?" I gasped. Ellie was much more free-spirited than I was.

"Hmmm, imagine what people would think?" Ellie giggled, delighted with herself.

"Not happening!" I responded. "Now then, what do you want? It's my turn to pay," I declared, conscious that Ellie had done me a favour and I hadn't exactly been gracious about thanking her.

"Well then," Ellie clapped her hands as a child might, "in that case, I'll have a chocolate milkshake and a piece of caramel shortbread, I think. It's too nice outside for a hot drink." And it was. Although it was only April, the sky was blue and the sun was shining, its warming rays chasing away the last vestiges of winter. "Oh, and by the way, I did an internet search for 'featherbedding' while you were with the doctor. It's an actual word, although it's nothing fun and certainly nothing that Blake would ever do to you."

"Hmmm," I answered, only half listening. "Go on then. What does it mean?"

"I can't remember exactly, but it was something about employment law. There were no feathers or any beds mentioned in any of the dictionary definitions I looked at." Ellie pulled a face, and I couldn't help but burst out laughing.

While we queued, I pulled my phone from my bag to text my dad. He was a worrier and had only agreed not to come to my appointment after I'd promised to text him as soon as I'd seen the doctor. As I went to unlock my device, I briefly caught sight of my grandmother's face reflected in the inky blackness of the lock screen. *Beware, Emma. Darkness surrounds you,* she whispered to me.

"Oh no," I muttered out loud. My stomach dropped to the floor before bouncing up to the ceiling, whereupon it gathered together a plague of ten thousand butterflies that proceeded to flutter around my insides.

"What?" Ellie asked, a large dollop of concern in her voice.

"I've just received a warning. My nan says I have to beware. Apparently darkness surrounds me, whatever that means," I muttered. Marvellous! I was just on the point of getting my life back after what had happened in February and now something else was going to ruin it. Was it too much to ask for five minutes worth of peace and quiet?

"Is that just because of who your beau is?" Ellie asked, scrunching up her brow.

"You know as much as I do," I replied, scowling at her.

"Try not to worry about it until later," Ellie offered, despite the fact that she was most definitely and very obviously worried about something herself. "A café is probably not the best place to start debating what your nan meant."

"Fine. How about much later? Like, after I've had my first date with Blake tonight," I finished sarcastically, taking my frustration out on Ellie while firing off a text to my dad.

Ellie smiled faintly but didn't comment.

It wasn't long before we were seated, people-watching while gorging on cake. In a bid to shake off my mood and not think about dire warnings of darkness, I focussed all of my thoughts on what I was eating and tried to forget everything else. My choice of dessert had been hot chocolate fudge cake, and the warm syrup melted in my mouth. The intense sweetness made me sigh with pleasure.

What's that? Blake asked suddenly. I hadn't exactly forgotten that he'd proven himself able to taste what I was eating, but his interruption still surprised me. I wondered if he could sense all reality through me or only taste and made a mental note to experiment further.

Chocolate cake, it's delicious, I taunted.

It does taste good, he replied. I half expected him to materialise, but he didn't. Immediately my suspicions were aroused. After nearly a thousand years of exclusion, Blake liked nothing better than to be a part of the world. However, no amount of wondering would clue me in to what he was up to because while he could read my thoughts, I could not read his.

"What do you make of that lady?" Ellie asked, gesturing towards a heavy-set, older woman who was elegantly in a knee-length black dress that she'd accessorised with what could have been a diamond necklace but was most likely a diamante one and skyscraper heels that I lusted after, having only been able to wear pumps for the last eight weeks. From what I could see as she paced backwards and forwards in the main foyer of the Vic, they were matte black with a textured finish and a pointed toe.

"I want her shoes." I sighed, somehow managing to box away my fears. Ellie's attempt to pull my thoughts away from a darker place had worked, for now at least.

"You and shoes." Ellie rolled her eyes. "You lust over them but rarely wear them. I bet you haven't even worn the ones that you bought in the Trafford Centre yet, have you?"

I huffed mournfully. "No, but I haven't been able to wear anything other than these," I answered, poking her in the shin under the table with my foot. "Maybe now that I can walk again, we can all go somewhere, me and Blake, you and Scott." I arched an eyebrow in her direction, ignoring the growing swell of discomfort in my abdomen. Apparently even when I suggested an outing, my nervous system didn't like it, but this was a conversation I'd been wanting to have for a while, and it would work quite nicely as a distraction technique, assuming I could forget what I'd just proposed.

"Me and Scott?" The pitch of Ellie's voice was raised ever so slightly above what was normal for her. Other people might have missed it, but I knew Ellie better than I knew myself.

"Come on, Ellie, when are you going to admit it to yourself? You're in love with him. And I'm fairly certain he's in love with you too. He's just too pig-headed to say anything about it."

"I don't—"

I stopped her from protesting. "You even genned up on the X-Men for heaven's sake." The advantage of having had a fractured ankle and surplus time off work was that I'd had a lot of spare time to reflect over the past few months, and as I'd played and replayed all of my earlier conversations with Blake, I'd remembered Ellie describing him as being like the Multiple Man. It was a fairly accurate description actually. Blake's purpose was to reap the souls of the dying, but his consciousness could only be in one place at once. In order to reap several souls at the same time, he was aided by unconscious 'copies' of himself. None of us really understood what the copies were; he didn't even know if he was responsible for creating them, and he certainly couldn't control them. All any of us knew for certain was that if he didn't choose to take a soul himself, a copy would step in.

I'd always known that Ellie had a thing for my brother, not that she'd ever spoken about it of course, I just knew. I'd seen the sideways glances and heard the pensive sighs. Personally I didn't get it, but when I tried to look at Scott through someone else's eyes, I was forced to admit that he was a handsome chappie. I just couldn't wrap my head around the idea of him being loveable.

Scott and I looked alike, but Scott was a blacksmith by trade. Whereas my height and weight made me look a little on the rounded side, his made him look like an Amazon god, an Amazon blacksmith god. If Amazon blacksmith gods had ever had unruly red hair, that was.

Ellie turned pink, but I pushed on, the discovery of my own soulmate had made me want the same for her. "I don't mind, you know. If you want to ask Scott out, that's okay."

"You think Scott's a pain."

"Well d'oh, he's my brother. Of course I think he's a pain. I also love the both of you and want you to be happy. I could wear my new shoes at your wedding!" I exclaimed, overjoyed at the idea.

"I think you're getting a little ahead of yourself." Ellie laughed. "And anyway, surely your bridesmaid dress would be purple?" Clearly she'd given the matter some thought. I filed that nugget of information away for another time.

"My shoes could be the accent colour," I declared, picturing the look. I would wear a satin, strapless gown in a dark shade of eggplant. It would have to be an A-line cut because I couldn't pull off anything too figure-hugging. And somehow it would be trimmed in a dusky shade of pink that would be an exact match to the colour of my new shoes, the ones I'd bought in the Trafford Centre. I hadn't figured out how the trimming would work yet though. Maybe a belt? Or a sash?

Ellie just shook her head. "What about that person over there?" She changed the subject back to the people around us.

"Oh no you don't. It's my turn," I answered, letting the subject of her and Scott drop . . . for now. "What about him?" I gestured to an older man sat in the corner of the coffee shop. He had a 1950s look about him. He was smartly dressed in a three-piece suit with a yellow silk tie at his neck and a fedora hat on his head.

"Him who?" Ellie asked, twisting in her seat to look exactly where I pointed.

"Don't you see him?" I asked. "Over there in the corner."

"Emma, there's no one there," Ellie answered grimly. Uh-oh, we'd been here before.

"This can't be happening again," I groaned, wilting in my seat.

"Maybe there's an explanation. Maybe you can see ghosts now that you're soulmates with Blake."

"What? Ghosts? Do you think they're a thing? And if they are, shouldn't I have been able to see them all along? Blake and I have been soulmates all along after all, we just didn't find each other until recently." I knew I was rambling, but I couldn't seem to stop myself.

"Hmmm, I guess. Maybe you could see them all along, though. Maybe you just didn't know what you were seeing?"

"Maybe . . ." I said, letting my thoughts wander. Had I seen ghosts all my life and not realised it? Was that a possibility? I racked my brains, searching my memory banks for anything that might have been classed as spooktacular from my childhood. Nothing stood out, but then again I'd never believed in the supernatural. Before all of this, before learning that the Grim Reaper was my soulmate, I didn't even believe in him, let alone in angels or demons and definitely not in the Tooth Fairy or Father Christmas. Ghosts had never even crossed my mind.

"Why don't you ask Blake?" Ellie suggested.

"Good idea," I said out loud. *Blake?* I said in the depths of my mind, once again casting my thought into the air.

What? Blake answered curtly. He sounded preoccupied.

Are ghosts a thing?

They're called remnants.

Ghosts, remnants . . . are they not one and the same?

No. Ghosts are . . .

Can you explain later? I interrupted, fairly sure that the explanation would be a long one. Blake was very precise with what he knew. *I'm with Ellie at the minute,* I explained, hoping to pacify him. *Are there many of them?*

Blake huffed, *I wouldn't know. They tend to avoid me. They will most likely avoid you too.*

They avoid you? Why?

How should I know?

"Well?" Ellie asked.

"Blake says they are called remnants. He also says they tend to avoid him."

"That's weird. And I see Mr. Particular is back."

"He never went away," I answered. "Dammit," I cursed, dismayed at how my day was unfolding and frustrated that I couldn't seem to catch a break. "This was supposed to be a good day," I whined. "I was supposed to be given the all-clear, have coffee with you, and then spend the night with Blake. I was not supposed to receive ominous warnings from my long-dead ancestors and find out that ghosts are a real thing. I mean, come on!"

Chapter 2 – Blake

Friday 12th April 2019

Blake was indeed standing on the rooftop of Blackpool's hospital. He could sense roughly where Emma was and so had followed her route from above, tracking her all the way to her appointment and then all the way back to the main entrance. It wasn't that he could always tell where she was, but the outpouring of emotion from her was so intense at the minute that he couldn't help but home in on it. She was like a radio signal broadcasting her whereabouts into the air. All he had to do was tune into the right frequency.

Just in the last few hours, he'd felt her anxiety rise and fall several times, spiking so sharply on occasion that it was like being punched in the gut. She'd been distressed ever since the attack. Blake was concerned, but he didn't understand the fear that radiated from within her. Her attacker, Peter Collins, was dead. Not only that but his soul was never going to be reborn ever again. Blake had made sure of that when he'd cleaved it in two, becoming judge, jury, and executioner for the first time in his life. Blake felt no guilt for his actions. Peter had threatened Emma's life, so Blake had taken his instead.

It didn't surprise him when Emma lingered in the main entrance of the Vic, indulging in one of her favourite pastimes, although he'd never understood why she thought of it as 'coffee and cake' when in actual fact she usually ordered a hot chocolate or a milkshake. Blake liked to be specific. Ordinarily he would have wanted to join her, but by the time his mouth exploded with the taste and texture of what she was eating, he was lost in thought. Absently he revelled in the fact that he could sometimes taste what Emma ate, but he didn't pursue the thought beyond that, he was too wrapped up in something else that was bothering him.

His only question was borne out of wanting to know exactly what she'd eaten so that he could sample it himself another time. *What's that?*

Chocolate cake, Emma replied. *It's delicious.*

It does taste good, Blake replied, but truthfully he was distracted. His own emotions were just as confusing as Emma's. He was simultaneously worried about her and irritated by her actions. Blake might have watched over mankind for almost a thousand years, but he'd been unprepared for what life was really like. The onslaught of sights, sounds, tastes, textures, sensations, and bewildering sentiments was . . . well, an onslaught.

How dare Emma forbid him from accompanying her to meet with the doctor? And annoyingly she'd put just enough will into what she'd said that he'd had no choice but to obey. Fury clawed at him, enticing him to abandon reason, but he did not want to be overtaken by such emotion again. He'd spent too much of his life angry as it was. It was difficult though; he was no one's pet, and he most certainly did not intend to be controlled by anyone, not even Emma.

In an effort to distract himself, Blake forced his thoughts away from his ire, consciously puzzling over something else. He'd come into being in 1027 and had lived for almost a thousand years by a defined set of rules. His purpose was to reap the souls of the dying, and all souls were reaped unless they'd turned dark, in which case they were subject to a cleaving. But Blake had never before been able to see souls, not when they'd been safely tucked away inside of a body anyway. He knew that there were some who claimed to be able to read auras and would confidently proclaim that everyone's soul had a unique colour pattern, but he'd always believed them to be a silvery, almost translucent colour, with the exception of those that had turned to the colour of soot.

Until recently, the only time he'd ever glimpsed a soul was when he'd watched a copy give the Kiss of Death on his behalf. As the copy drew away from the embrace, there was a brief moment when the soul was visible, just for a second, while it was being pulled from its carrier and before it eventually settled within him. That had changed on the night that Emma had been attacked.

Blake found the memories of that night to be distasteful. While standing in a field by a deserted country lane, an *almost* deserted country lane, he'd seen two souls burning brightly in the vicinity. One had been the half of his soul that Emma carried; it had gleamed golden in colour. The other had been mostly silver, but it had been darkened by an oily black stain that was tinged with differing hues of red. At the time, Blake had been so focussed on what was happening to Emma that he hadn't stopped to think about what he was seeing, the souls of Emma and Peter, rather than their outward appearances. It was only in recent weeks that the thought had occurred. And eventually he'd discovered, quite by accident, that if he focussed his thoughts on Emma and looked through people instead of at them, he could see their souls. The living lit up!

Emma's soul—his soul—was the colour of a sunbeam. To call it golden belittled it, although truthfully there was no other word that would suffice. While it did have a golden hue, it sparkled and shimmered as though Emma was the source of all light. It looked like the crystal-clear blue seas of the Caribbean at dawn, just as the sun rose up from the depths of the ocean and its rays caught on the surface of the water. And, as he'd always believed, most other souls did look like a translucent form of liquid silver, but some were tinged with that oily black stain he'd seen on Peter's soul. Blake's nostrils flared at the mere thought of such souls, reminded as he was of Emma's attacker. He surmised that people afflicted in this way were currently engaged in an internal battle between good and evil. Perhaps if the person transformed themselves, their soul would be washed clean, but if not, at the end of their life, Blake would let the soul in question rise up from the body before striking it down with his weapon.

Blake's weapon—or scythe—was a metal blade that stood atop a long, stout wooden pole. It curved in a graceful arc that narrowed to a point approximately two feet away from the handle. It was made of a substance unknown to modern man, the most robust substance in all of existence, and had been polished and then polished some more before being blessed by a type of magic that Blake knew nothing about. Blake had no idea who'd forged the weapon, or when. He'd simply pulled it from the ether the first time he'd needed it. Before meeting Emma, he'd only ever used it on a soul that was all the way black, and he'd never intervened in life-or-death moments. But he'd saved Emma's life by condemning that of her attacker before destroying his soul. He hadn't even known that he could judge people unworthy until that moment.

Blake's thoughts turned to what was really bothering him. He stood staring across the coastal town of Blackpool and out to the sea, thinking about the two souls that didn't conform to the standard, the souls of Ellie and her mother, Joanne. From them a bright blue light pulsated.

"Seith," Blake called for the only companion he'd ever known, his voice quiet and even. He could have screamed Seith's name without any fear of being overheard if he'd wanted to do so, but there was no need. Seith always came when Blake called and, sure enough, was by his side almost instantaneously without any theatrics.

Blake suspected that Seith knew more than he did about certain things. Seith certainly behaved like an older, wiser sibling, one that was determined to let Blake find things out for himself and make his own mistakes. Blake felt the embers of his temper heating up again and sighed his annoyance. "Can you see the souls of man?" he asked, turning to look Seith in the eye.

Seith stared back with amber-coloured eyes that gleamed brightly in the sunlight before replying in a way that surprised Blake. Finally, he'd found something that he could do and Seith could not.

Chapter 3 – Emma

Friday 12th April 2019

It was finally happening! After sixty-one days as a couple (counting from when we first had sex because when else do you count from when your other half is an incorporeal being), Blake and I were going on our first date. We'd never really been out together; in fact our one and only social outing had been to Grammy's funeral and that didn't really count. Since then, it had been easier to stay at home snuggled up in the safety of my little two-up two-down. Don't get me wrong, we'd been to my parents' house a couple of times and plenty of people had been round. In fact, I'd had an endless slew of visitors in the last few weeks, not that they'd all been introduced to Blake, mind you. But we hadn't actually been out despite Blake wanting to experience all that life had to offer. There just hadn't been the time. And no, I wasn't afraid to be out there, out in the big, bad, wide world, but I'd had other things on my mind and I hadn't really seen the point of squeezing in a date. Eventually Blake had worn me down, and now I was really rather excited. In fact, my stomach churned at the thought of what was to come later on this evening, but that was perfectly normal. Okay . . . I'll admit it, I was a little bit nervous as well but only in the way that anyone else would have been. Tonight was a big deal.

Blake had been given strict instructions to stay away for the afternoon so that I could get ready in the peace and quiet of my own home, and so that he could knock for me as any other gentleman caller would. Well, not exactly as any other gentleman caller would because Blake would have no choice but to materialise out of thin air, and he couldn't exactly do that in the street. He also couldn't fetch me flowers or chocolates or even pay for the meal because of the aforementioned incorporeal being restriction, but I didn't care. We were going on a date, and that was supposed to be exciting, so that was what it was!

As all ladies will know, as a general rule of thumb, the older you get, the less time you take getting ready. But I was consciously ignoring my nan's warning, so I spent most of the afternoon preparing myself for what was to come. First of all, there was the 'deciding what to wear' stage, which was complicated by the fact that I still couldn't manage in heels. Having not put any weight on my ankle in the last eight weeks, it felt odd to use it again, and I was a smidge on the cautious side. It felt a strange thing to admit, but I no longer trusted one of my own body parts, and so my going-out shoes were off the table. That left me with some trainers (all of which were too plain or too scruffy), some flip-flop-type sandals (the weather was nice but not that nice), or some sparkly pumps that shredded my heels every time I wore them. The pumps it was then.

With my footwear chosen, I turned my attention to the rest of my attire. Eventually I settled on a denim skirt because jeans felt too casual and all of my other skirts absolutely-most-definitely needed me to be in shoes that had at least a little lift. I paired the skirt with a boat-neck, grey T-shirt-type top that had three-quarter length sleeves and was embellished with tiny crystals scattered across the front in a star-shaped pattern. By the time my outfit was decided upon, there were clothes strewn across the whole of my bedroom, but at least I had something acceptable picked out to wear. And then I moved onto the 'hair and makeup' stage.

Blake had only ever seen me in my about-the-house attire. I wanted him to be blown away when he saw me and that required effort on my behalf. Rather than leaving my hair in its usual ponytail, I carefully shampooed it while in the shower. And I used the 'good stuff,' the expensive stuff that I only ever used on special occasions because my budget didn't run to using it on a regular basis. It smelled divine and left my hair so soft. After I'd blow-dried it, I pinned it back into a loose bun, pulling two or three tendrils loose to frame my face. And then I turned my attention to my makeup. Quite frankly, I didn't have the courage to dress my eyes in the way that I really wanted to, but I did use eyeliner and some neutral-coloured eyeshadows to create a mostly pleasing look before applying a coat of mascara. A bit of lip gloss, my clothes, and then that was me done.

"Well, Watson, what do you think?" I said to the only one of my cats that was in the bedroom with me, doing a little twirl for his benefit. He lay at the bottom of my bed, curled up into a ball with his tail wrapped around his body. "I know it's not what I normally wear," I continued speaking when he blatantly ignored me, "but I wanted to make an effort. This is our first date after all." Butterflies erupted in my tummy as I said the words 'first date.' "Idiot," I muttered to myself, trying to shrug off my doubts.

I plonked myself down on the bed next to Watson and curled my body around his before stroking him softly. "Oh Watson, what if it's a disaster? What if we've got nothing to talk about? It's not like we met under normal circumstances. What if he doesn't like me in the real world?" I asked, not that he replied of course. He didn't even bat an eyelid. "I know, I know, you want to be left alone to snooze. Okay, okay, I get it." I lifted my body from around his before leaning over to kiss his head, breathing deeply as I did so to inhale his scent. When I pulled away, there was a wet spot where I'd obviously drooled on him.

"Oops, sorry, Watson." I giggled, stroking him once more.

Sitting fully upright, I glanced down and saw a red stain on the palm of my hand. "What the . . .?" I asked, touching Watson's head again. He didn't seem to be injured in any way. Confused, I lifted my hand to my face and discovered that it was in fact my blood, not Watson's.

"A nosebleed! Blimey, I can't remember the last time I had one of those." I reached for a tissue, pulling several from a box that had been dumped by the side of my bed some weeks previously. Were you meant to lean back or sit with your head between your knees when your nose leaked bodily fluids? I couldn't remember and so opted for sitting relatively upright with a handful of tissues pressed up against my nostrils. My blood had a sharp metallic smell that tickled the back of my throat.

While I sat there, my mind wandered back to what I'd been asking Watson. Ultimately my fears could be summed up in one question, what if Blake were only with me because he had no other choice? As far as I was aware, Blake and I sort of had to be together because we shared a soul and because if Blake wasn't with me . . . well, then he wasn't with anyone. My rogue thought made my stomach drop all of a sudden. There was no denying that my attraction to him was absolute; I'd been drawn to him from the very beginning. And I was fairly certain that he found me easy on the eye, even though I didn't understand why, but perhaps he found me boring. Perhaps, if he had a choice, he'd prefer to be with someone else? Someone more fun-loving like Ellie?

There's no one else I'd prefer to be with. Blake's voice cut through the noise in my head.

Blake! Where are you? I exclaimed.

On the roof of a house two or three doors down from yours.

What on earth are you doing up there?

You asked me to stay away.

Well, yes, but I expected you to be somewhere else. America, Australia, China, anywhere really.

There's nowhere else I want to be. I'm playing by your rules, I'm far enough away so as not to be in your bubble or to watch you get ready, but I'm close enough to hear your thoughts.

You were listening?

We've had this conversation before as I recall. How do you not hear a sound?

Much as I would never ever admit it, certainly not out loud anyway, Blake was right. He couldn't *not* hear my thoughts when he was within earshot. It was just frustrating that 'within earshot' for him was a little different than it was for anyone else, and he could listen to my innermost thoughts as well the words that I said out loud. *Hmmm,* I replied, unwilling to confess that I accepted his rationale, my thoughts bouncing back to what had been worrying me before Blake had so rudely interrupted.

Emma, Blake stopped me again. *Even before I knew who you were or that you enabled me to be physically present, I longed for you. Do not doubt my love for you.*

You love me? I asked, shocked. Neither Blake nor I had said the L-word. I mean, I'd thought about it, but we'd only been together for a few weeks. Was it possible to fall for someone that quickly? Until recently if you'd have asked me my thoughts on such things, I'd have scoffed. How could you possibly be in love with someone without really knowing them? And you couldn't get to know someone without spending time with them, a lot of time. Love needed to grow as you developed shared passions and a friendship based on trust. But I craved Blake with every fibre of my being. Was that love?

"I thought you knew," Blake answered, pulling me to my feet and enfolding me in his arms, taking it upon himself to intrude in person. "You can sense my emotions."

I laid my head on the satin lapels of his jacket before answering, grateful that the tissues I'd been holding to my nose had fallen to the floor. "Well, yes, but . . ." My words trailed off into nothing.

Blake reached up and gently placed a finger under my chin, using it as leverage to tilt my face towards his. He placed the most delicate of kisses on my lips, lingering but not pushing for anything more. His dominant hand remained between us while we kissed, but his other one slid down my back to my waist whereupon he pulled me closer to him. My own hands explored his body, taking in the texture of his perfectly tailored jacket. I toyed with its hem before reaching underneath to run my fingers around the waistband of his trousers. The material felt odd to my touch; I'd been expecting jeans, but he was wearing something that felt more like a high-quality brushed cotton.

"What are you wearing?" I asked, breaking away from his embrace to look at him properly. "Oh my," I breathed. Blake always looked stunning, but dressed in an exquisite tuxedo . . . he took my breath away.

"Do I look suitable?" Blake asked.

I couldn't help but laugh. "Oh Blake." Not only did I see the injured look on his face, but I felt his wounded pride uncurling like a spring inside of me. It quickly turned to annoyance, and I knew that if I didn't intervene, our first date was going to be a disaster. "Blake, you look so handsome, but we're only going to the pub."

"We're going on a date, aren't we? This is appropriate, isn't it?"

"Oh honey." I didn't normally use terms of endearment, but Blake looked so crestfallen. I bit my lip, not wanting to hurt his feelings but decided to press on, knowing that public embarrassment would be worse for him. "Not exactly. Tuxedos are only worn to formal events. Maybe if we were going to a ball or the theatre, but not the pub. Look through your stolen memories," I encouraged.

When Blake reaped (or cleaved) a soul, he saw the life that had been lost, so I knew that he had plenty of material to review. It didn't take long before he'd seen enough. "I'll change," he announced, disappearing in the same breath. Blake's outward appearance was essentially nothing more than a manifestation of what he believed himself to look like, ergo he could 'reset' his look whenever and however he liked, as long as he wasn't constrained by my bubble.

While he was gone, I took the opportunity to reapply my lip gloss and gather up a jacket, a lightweight scarf, my purse, phone, and house keys. I was downstairs when Blake reappeared, and my heart stopped dead. One minute, it was beating away quite happily, and the next, I may as well have been a corpse.

"Huh," was all I managed to get out. Blake was easy on the eye in a tuxedo but dressed in snug jeans that tightly cupped his, ah . . . bottom and a plain white shirt edged in blue, he was beyond beautiful. Simple words could not adequately express the bow wave of lust that swept over me.

"What? Is this still not right?" Blake huffed.

I couldn't reply because the wind had been stolen from my lungs (although at least my heart was beating again, it was just beating a little frenetically). Instead, I concentrated on my emotions and pushed them outwards toward Blake so that he could feel what I was feeling. Slowly a hint of a smile ghosted his lips. He looked so sexy that my id was screaming at me to scrap the idea of a first date and head straight back to the bedroom. Only the fact that Blake had been pestering me to go out for a while now persuaded me to put my libido on hold.

"We should, erm . . . go then," I finally said, although the butterflies that had erupted in my innards earlier now played tag with each other inside of me. But that was understandable because I was going on a date. Somewhere, in one of the deepest, darkest, most cavern-like corners of my mind, a small voice was trying to tell me that my emotional distress had nothing to do with going on a date and everything to do with going out, but I stubbornly ignored it. Yes, I'd felt queasy leaving the house ever since . . . well, you know, but there was always a logical reason for my nerves. Take this morning's excursion as an example: my anxiety had only been because of what the doctor might say. There was absolutely nothing else going on.

Our walk to the pub was relatively pleasant; we linked arms and ambled along, saying very little to each other. Personally, I was still reeling from the L-bomb that Blake had dropped (nothing else!), and he seemed content to let the evening play out as any other date would. When I focussed on his emotions rather than my own, an image of a cat lapping at a saucer of cream came to mind. He was content to be in this place, at this time, with me. As we neared the pub, a gentle breeze nipped at my ankles, causing a shiver to run up my spine. I picked up the pace until the pub hooved into view.

The Sparrowhawk, my local, was a short walk through the village. It was an old coach house that had been converted hundreds of years previously but had been recently renovated. A polished wooden bar ran down the length of the building standing on top of a mottled golden-grey stone floor. Opposite the bar, enormous picture windows captured the last rays of sunshine, bouncing the light off the whitewashed walls so that the place felt spacious despite the low ceiling. The décor was minimalistic with very few paintings or pictures, and I was yet to find any reference to the sparrowhawk that the pub was named after. Its food was relatively simple, burger and chips rather than coq au vin, but it was nice, filling, and relatively inexpensive, which was essential bearing in mind I'd be paying the bill at the end of the night.

Blake had never yet had alcohol. His anticipation had been mounting with every step we'd taken, so after I'd discreetly glanced at all of the other patrons to make sure none of them rubbed up against my weirdo-radar, I quickly ordered us a bottle of Malbec and found a table by the window. Almost before our bums were in their seats, Blake had taken a huge swig of his wine.

"Blake!" I chastised. "We tend to sip our drinks."

"You sip it because you've had it before. You've had the luxury of being able to do everything you've ever wanted. I, on the other hand, have not. It tastes funny, doesn't it?" He wrinkled his nose. "People consume a lot of this, but I think I prefer juice."

"You didn't give it time to breathe. What did you expect?" I swirled the liquid around in my glass before taking a sip, barely wetting my lips. "Mmm, it's a good one." I offered an opinion as though I was an expert in wine but really, what did I know? I'd read that a good Malbec had top notes of plum resting on an oak palette, but in the supermarket my choice was based on how pretty the label was or if it were on offer. Three for a tenner was the magic phrase! "What shall we talk about?" I asked.

"I thought dates were about getting to know each other. Tell me everything."

"That would take all night." I laughed, relaxing into our date, finally feeling safe because Blake was with me. What could possibly go wrong with the Grim Reaper by my side? "Besides, you know everything there is to know about me already. I know next to nothing about you. You've been everywhere, seen everything. Tell me about it."

"Me?" Blake said, his top lip curling into a sneer as if the words left a sour taste in his mouth. "My life has been nothing more than an existence. Yes, I've been everywhere and I've seen a lot of things, but I was not allowed to join in with any of them. I've had no one to share my life with."

"You had Seith," I replied as gently as I could. The depth of Blake's emotion was a little overwhelming. His jealousy towards mankind far surpassed anything I'd ever experienced. No wonder he'd lost interest in people. It had either been that or go insane with envy.

"To a degree," Blake finally admitted. "Seith was . . ." Blake paused. "I don't even know who or what Seith is. My guardian? Why would I need a guardian?" Blake fell silent.

"Why don't we just talk about normal first date stuff?" I suggested before Blake lost himself to what he was feeling. Between my own emotional distress (that I was doing my utmost to ignore) and his, it was too much to bear.

"Such as?" he arched an eyebrow in my direction.

"Do you read books?"

"No."

"You can read, though, can't you?" The question just popped out.

"Of course I can read." Blake sniffed and glared at me, his eyes narrowing ever so slightly. Oops, I'd obviously hit a nerve. "I can't turn the pages," he explained curtly.

Moving swiftly on, I thought, not really thinking about the fact that Blake could hear my thoughts. "What about movies? Have you ever watched a film?" I asked.

"Have I?" Blake beamed at me. It was rare to see him smile with such gay abandon, and my heart skipped a beat. Phew! "I was at the first showing of a moving picture."

"Wow, really? When was that?"

"1865."

"Huh, I didn't know that cinema was so old."

"It isn't. Cinematography only started evolving in the early 1900s. It became popular in the 1930s."

"Do you go often?"

Blake inclined his head. "I enjoy the cinema. No need to touch anything, and no risk of the channel being turned over halfway through a film. It's a good way of passing time."

"What's your favourite film then?" I grinned, finally feeling like I was on solid ground and enjoying the fact that I was seeing a whole new side of him. Why hadn't we talked about anything normal in the last eight weeks? Oh yes, because we'd been in bed for most of it. I was recovering, and then we were, erm . . . well, we were getting to know each other in a different way.

"Good question . . ." Blake paused clearly giving the matter some thought. "*Meet Joe Black,*" he finally answered.

"That's about a grim reaper."

"I'm aware. I like the fact that Brad Pitt plays me."

"It's not actually about you, you know?"

"I know. What's yours?"

"*50 First Dates,*" I answered without missing a beat. Who didn't like a film with cute penguins in it? "Or maybe *How To Train Your Dragon,*" I added, cocking my head to one side as indecision caught hold of me. "Toothless reminds me of Cooper."

After that, the conversation flowed easily between us, and it wasn't until much later that I suddenly yawned.

"Time to go?" Blake asked.

"Yes, I think so," I answered.

That pesky breeze from earlier tickled the back of my ankles as I stood up. Other than that, though, there was no warning of what was about to happen. Suddenly the tiny tealight on our table flared into life. The flame, which had barely flickered all evening, doubled in height and then doubled again. It spat embers in every direction, onto the pine table, onto the stone floor, onto the gauze curtains that were neatly tied to one side of the window, onto my hand. I winced, rubbing at the burn mark, and scrambled back from the table.

Those sparks that landed on solid surfaces sizzled out into nothing, leaving only sooty marks behind as evidence that anything had happened, but those that landed on fabric quickly turned into an inferno that climbed higher and higher in search of more fuel to consume.

Blake was at my side faster than I would have thought possible. He pulled me away from the misbehaving candle and the growing gaggle of flames. "What the . . ." I started to say, but my voice was drowned out by the commotion that erupted around us. It wasn't just our candle that had suddenly exploded, seemingly every candle in the room had done the same and there were growing fires all around us.

"Out!" I heard someone sound the alarm as the blaze grew higher. "Out! Everybody get out!"

Blake wasted no time, he grabbed my hand and ploughed for the door. I barely had time to snatch up my bag before he had me out of the building and in the carpark. "We should go," he said urgently.

"We can't, Blake. We'll have to talk to the police."

"As far as they're concerned, I don't exist."

"People have seen us; we can't just leave. In fact, you should go back in and help people, see if you can rescue anyone."

"I can't, not without you by my side, and you're not going back in there." He had a point, and while I wanted to believe that I was the kind of person who would dive willingly into a burning building to save others, I found out in that moment that I was not. Instead, I allowed myself to be commanded by him because fear had me clutched tightly within its grip, grasping at me with its cold fingers, threatening to overwhelm me. I didn't want to poke about in my psyche in a bid to understand the cause of the fear, so I stood passively at Blake's side watching the newly renovated Sparrowhawk burn.

Blake, sensing my mixed emotions, pulled me into his side and took my hand in his. I'd never thought of myself as dainty or small, but Blake had a remarkable talent for making me feel wonderfully petite.

More and more people joined us, and as a sad little group, we watched the building as it was rapidly engulfed in flames. The fire spread quickly, hungrily eating away at the innards of the building, presumably fed by the wooden furniture, the lustrous fabric at the windows, and the alcohol.

"Will anyone die?" I whispered to Blake.

"Yes," he replied, his voice gruff.

"What is it?" I asked, stepping to one side and looking up at him. As usual, his face was unreadable.

"You know that I am drawn to death . . ." he started to explain. He was, he could literally feel it when someone had any chance of dying in the near future, and he could also tell how likely it was to happen depending on their actions (or the actions of those around them). "No one was slated to die here tonight until after the fire started. I should have been able to sense it before then. It was . . . unnatural."

I didn't know what to say to that, so I kept my mouth shut. How could a fire be described as unnatural? Horrible, yes, but fire was a natural phenomenon. Although, neither one of us had knocked the candle, so how had it happened? Tealights didn't normally cause so much bother. I used them all the time at home without any trouble. And it was odd that all of them had misbehaved at the same time. Besides which, why hadn't Blake been able to predict the fire? I started to get the feeling that I was standing on the edge of a precipice with no way back and only one way down. Something bad was coming. I just didn't know what it was.

Some of my questions were echoed by the police later on but thankfully nothing came of their inquiries because several diners all told the same story, the candles seemingly came to life all on their own and decided to burn down the pub.

Chapter 4 – Emma

Saturday 13ᵗʰ April 2019

It felt like my eyes had only just closed when a jackhammer obnoxiously decided it was time for me to get up. "Urgh," I groaned, lifting my head just enough to pull the pillow out from under it.

"It's Ellie," Blake supplied.

"It's still dark," I mumbled from underneath the pillow, which I'd repositioned and pulled down tightly against my ears.

"She won't go away."

"Bollocks." I sighed, relinquishing my hold on the bedding that I'd been using to keep the day at bay.

Sure enough, the knocking continued. Throwing back the covers, I dragged myself out of bed and trudged down the stairs. With a sigh, I opened the door. "You have a key," I remarked, glaring at Ellie. She didn't answer but instead flung herself at me and wrapped me in a hug.

"Oh my God, Emma," she eventually said, without letting me go. "I can't believe what happened to you last night."

"Hmph." I was starting to regret the text I'd sent, filling her in. "Again I say, you have a key," I muttered, although I did hug her back. It wasn't Ellie's fault that I'd barely slept after all.

"I know, but now that Blake has moved in, I thought I ought to knock."

"Blake hasn't moved in," I argued, breaking away from her and stepping back into the relative warmth of my house. Bearing in mind it was early-o-clock in the morning and I'd been standing on my front doorstep in nothing but a pair of cotton pyjamas, I was turning blue with cold.

Ellie followed, closing the front door behind her. "Uh-huh, he spends pretty much every night here."

"Well, yes, but . . ."

"And he doesn't have a home of his own."

"True, but . . ."

"So, that suggests he's moved in with you."

"I suppose, but . . . ." First the L-word and now this. My head was starting to hurt. Didn't I have enough on my plate already? "Whatever," I eventually agreed. "Use your key in the future though. I was still in bed."

"So I see. Why don't you go and have a quick shower and I'll make breakfast? Your hair still smells smoky." She wrinkled her nose and headed off into the kitchen.

Seeing no reason to argue, I trudged back upstairs.

"Ellie's making breakfast," I said to Blake as I got to the top of stairs, before heading straight into the bathroom to make myself presentable.

Despite knowing that both Ellie and Blake were waiting, I took my time in the shower, letting the scalding hot water ease the tension in my shoulders. Ellie's comment about my hair had made me feel dirty, and so I scrubbed my hair twice before conditioning it, even though I'd only washed it with the good stuff the night before. After that, I scoured every inch of my skin until I was red raw, all the while replaying Ellie's words on a loop. *Now that Blake has moved in . . . Now that Blake has moved in . . . Now that Blake has moved in . . .*

Had Blake somehow moved in without me noticing? And what was it about that fact that bothered me? I loved Blake . . . didn't I? I was almost certain that I did, it's just . . . well, I'd never believed in love at first sight. Love needed time to flourish . . . didn't it? I certainly pined for Blake when he was absent, and I felt safer when he was with me. So, if he had moved in, that was a good thing, right? It wasn't like he took up much room, he didn't need any closet space and he hadn't got any manky pieces of furniture that he insisted on putting in the lounge. He hadn't even got a rogue pile of books to squeeze in among my own. It was just . . . surely if he had moved in, I would have been the first to know about it. I should have asked him if he actually wanted to move in with me. I should have given him a key. Shit! I should have given him a key. My heart rate jumped until I remembered that I was being a dumbass; Blake didn't need a key.

My headache grew steadily worse until I decided that enough was enough, for today at least. I stepped out from under the water and turned off the tap. "Oh well, I might as well get it over with," I grumbled to myself, looking into the mirror while wrapping a towel around me, securing it just above my boobs. I was fully expecting one of my ancestors to be waiting, but no one showed up despite my nan's dire warning. "You're joking, aren't you?" I continued with my griping. "When I don't want you, you're there full of doom and gloom, but when

I actually do want you, you won't come out and play. I could do with a little more than 'darkness surrounds you.' What the hell does that even mean?"

"Emma!" Ellie shouted from downstairs, interrupting my ranting. Perhaps she'd heard and decided to put a stop to it before I succeeded in working myself up into a self-induced fury. "Breakfast is nearly ready. You're going to want to eat it while it's hot."

Hot? I thought. *What the hell has she cooked?* As far as I knew, I had nothing in. The intrigue got me moving, and I quickly brushed my teeth, pulled my hair into a tight (wet) bun, and got dressed, opting for some plain black jog-bottoms and a grey hoodie.

"Seriously?" Ellie asked when I appeared in the kitchen-diner and sat myself at the dining table. "Is that what you're wearing to Cedar's?"

"Eh?"

"We're going to Cedar's this morning, aren't we?"

"I forgot," I answered honestly. "Maybe we should delay?"

Ellie turned from the cooker to face me. "No, I don't think that's a good idea."

I pulled a face before changing the subject. "Fine. What's for breakfast and where's Blake?"

"He left. He said to tell you that he wouldn't be far away."

"Hmmm," I remarked before mentally calling for Blake.

I'm on the roof, he answered. *Ellie gave me bacon.*

You didn't have to leave.

I know, but you're going out.

Blake wasn't being overly communicative. "You didn't ask him to go, did you?" My suspicions were aroused.

"No, I told him he was welcome to stay if he wanted, but he's still happier when it's just you." That was true, but I had a different opinion on what might have chased him away.

Did you hear what I was thinking about?

I did.

Shit! "So, where did you get the bacon from?" I asked, unable to follow up with Blake, unsure how I would even begin to explain what I was feeling when I didn't understand it myself.

Ellie set a plate down in front of me before answering. On it were two fluffy white bread rolls, each generously filled with several pieces of crispy bacon. "I brought it with me. Red or brown?"

"Red."

Ellie rolled her eyes but dutifully retrieved the tomato ketchup from the kitchen. Of course, she also set the brown sauce down next to it before turning back to make tea. Us Brits can't have a bacon butty without a good cup of tea!

Eventually she also sat at the table with me. We ate our sandwiches in silence for a couple of minutes before Ellie started firing questions in my direction. "So, how was your date? And what the hell happened? What did the police say? And ya know . . ." she faked an American accent, " . . . did you get up to any mischief when you got home?" Her eyes sparkled with glee.

It was my turn to roll my eyes. "It was perfect. I don't really know; it was weird. Pretty much what you'd expect. And to be honest, no."

"No," Ellie exclaimed in mock horror, shaking her head in disbelief before taking another bite of her sandwich, which she'd poisoned with brown sauce. Urgh.

"Ellie?" I asked, mulling over how to ask my next question. "What does it feel like when you're around my brother?"

Ellie nearly choked on her breakfast before muttering something about it being too early in the morning for such random questions, even though she was the one who'd rudely woken me at the crack of dawn.

"Come on, Ellie, I want to know. You do love him, don't you?"

It took Ellie a while to answer, but eventually she admitted it. "Okay, yes," she finally said, blushing a rosy-pink colour, which only served to accentuate the blue of her eyes. It didn't seem to matter what emotion flickered across Ellie's face, she was never anything less than gorgeous. "I've never actually thought it through until yesterday, but yes, I do love him. In fact, I think I've always been in love with him. There, I've said it." She looked proud of herself.

"So, what does it feel like? How do you know?"

"Emma!"

"What?" I asked with a straight face. Ellie has literally no boundaries when she was the one asking the questions. Today it was my turn.

"We're talking about your brother; do you really want to know what I think about?"

It was my turn to be embarrassed, but unlike Ellie, my face didn't glow pleasantly, it turned a bright scarlet colour instead. I wouldn't put it past her to get very explicit about her thought process. Oh God, what if she started talking about the size of his, erm . . . hands?

"Let's agree that certain parts of his anatomy are not to be referenced, shall we?"

"Why are you asking me anyway? You must know what it feels like to be in love."

"Do I?"

"Oh, come on, Emma, you're absolutely smitten."

"Well, yes, but I've only known Blake for a couple of months, maybe that's just lust."

Ellie laughed and shook her head. "I see the way you look at him, it's not just lust. Try and imagine your life without him or think about something bad happening to him." Ellie paused while I thought about what she'd said. A shudder rippled through my body. "See, you love him," she finished.

"What if that's just my half of the soul reacting to his half of the soul?"

"So what if it is?"

"Surely if it's love there should be more to it than that."

"Emma, seriously, honey. Stop worrying about everything and nothing. If Blake makes you happy, let him make you happy. Just enjoy being with him."

"I suppose," I muttered. I wanted to agree wholeheartedly with her but a lifetime of pre-conceived notions was hard to part with. "Ellie," I changed the subject, "do you think something odd is happening again?"

"Like what?"

"Well, it's just . . . I've never seen candles behave like that before. It was almost as though they came to life, all at the same time. And the flames really did take hold. It was awful, I just can't believe it. I can't believe someone died."

"It's very sad."

"It's more than sad, though; Blake said it was unnatural. He didn't sense anyone's death until after the fire started."

"Well, isn't that how his psychic ability works?"

"No, the possibility of a fire should have been in that person's future all along. But it came out of nowhere. Besides which, even if it was just a fire and I was just unlucky, there's still the issue of my nan's ominous warning."

"Well, yes, there is that. What do you think it means?"

"I've no idea. I don't think it's just because of Blake though."

"No, me either. But what else could it be? I'm fairly certain you've not attracted the attentions of another stalker in the last few weeks; you've barely left the house."

"I've left the house," I argued.

"Hardly. And never on your own."

"I went to Grammy's funeral. And I've been to Mum and Dad's. And all of my hospital appointments."

"But not to mine or Cedar's," Ellie argued back.

"Well, no, but only because I've not been able to drive since . . . well, you know, so you've always come to me."

"If you say so." Ellie arched her eyebrows, leaving me with the distinct impression that she didn't believe me, but before I could object any further—and believe me, I wanted to—she stood up and started clearing away. "Are you getting changed then or are you going out like that?"

"I'm going like this," I declared. It was childish, but I was annoyed with Ellie and as payback I'd decided that she'd just have to accept me in my scruffs.

"Perfect! You look beautiful." Ellie had a knack of raining on my parade.

I sighed. "I'll just go and get my shoes." What I really wanted to do was go back to bed and curl into a little ball and close my eyes and start this day all over again. Or maybe even this whole year. But that wasn't going to happen. Ellie had decided we were going to Cedar's, and so we were going to Cedar's. Even my untimely death wouldn't stop her. In the event of anything unfortunate happening, I was convinced that she'd simply take my corpse with her for coffee and cake with the gang. Such was Ellie's determination that I was leaving the house and mingling with other people.

Cedar's Veterinary Centre hadn't changed one iota while I'd been absent from work. Well, one thing had changed: Jessica and Fletcher, the practice kittens, had grown an astonishing amount!

"They're so big now," I cooed. At four months old, they were in the gangly phase of their development, with little fluffy bodies and long spindly legs. They'd come running when I'd pushed open the door to the break room, and so I'd scooped them both up. Obviously I preferred to think that they were happy to see me, but in all honesty they'd probably been trying to escape their prison. Until they were six months old, they were confined to the break room and the little apartment above the veterinary practice.

While I fussed the kittens, Ellie rounded up all the staff who were onsite and then flicked the kettle on to boil.

Andrew (the practice owner and our head vet) was the first to envelop me in a hug. He was quickly followed by Rhona and then Gary. Among the hugs, kisses, and general greetings, Jessica and Fletcher were deposited onto one of the armchairs where they promptly started fighting with each other. They might have grown, but I was heartened to see their dispositions were still the same.

"Charlotte and Tori are just finishing off a surgery," Ellie supplied as she continued to make a round of tea.

"It's great to see you," Rhona gushed. "When are you coming back to work?"

"Well, if Andrew says it's okay, I thought I'd aim for next week," I answered, despite the churning in my stomach. I simply had to go back to work; I had bills to pay. "Now that I've got the all-clear from the doctor, I can be put back on the rota." I glanced at Andrew but smiled at Gary, who, as the business manager, was responsible for allocating shifts.

"If the doctor says it's okay . . ." Andrew looked at Ellie, who nodded in agreement ". . . then it's okay with me." Apparently my boss knew me all too well.

"Awesome!" Gary was an absolute whizz at business, but he was more than just a great coordinator, marketing guru, finance expert, and commercial manager. He was also an outdoor enthusiast with an attitude (and the lingo) to match. He was one of those guys who had a perpetually tanned face and forearms.

The five of us had been chatting for a while, catching up on everything and nothing, when Charlotte and Tori entered. Tori beamed from ear-to-ear at the sight of me, but Charlotte hung back.

"Emma!" Tori grinned even harder. "It is sooo good to see you without those crutches. Urgh, I still have nightmares about what happened to you. It was awful." She reached up to hug me. Tori was an elf hiding in plain sight; she was so petite that even Ellie looked big standing next to her. Where Ellie was pale-skinned and blonde, though, Tori was dark with an olive complexion and jet-black hair that was tinged pink at its ends. Next week it could well be dip-dyed blue or green, though, you just couldn't tell with Tori. When not in work, she was always dressed in black with full goth makeup.

"I certainly wouldn't want to go through it again," I agreed with her, ignoring the fact that she had nightmares. Surely I was the only one allowed to have nightmares because of what had happened? "Hi, Charlotte," I changed the subject, smiling faintly in Charlotte's direction.

"Hi," she replied but didn't follow up with a hug. I couldn't blame her, I wasn't all that good at hiding my feelings, and she probably sensed that I'd never warmed to her. "I, erm . . . I'm having a cocktail party on Friday if you want to come. I've already invited Ellie. I don't know if she passed on the message."

"I haven't actually. I didn't forget, though, I just thought you might like to ask her yourself," Ellie answered.

What's she up to? I wondered as Gary spoke up. "Yay! A cocktail party."

"Oh, sorry, Gary, it's ladies only." Charlotte quirked her face.

"Awww maaan," Gary moaned.

"So, shall I tick you off as coming?" Charlotte asked me.

"Erm, yeah sure, that would be lovely, thanks." There wasn't a great deal else I could say with everyone hanging out together, but I had absolutely no intention of going to Charlotte's. I'd all but accused her of stalking me back in February, although I didn't know if she knew that. I'd even told the police my suspicions. How could I face her? I tuned out the chatter and studied her covertly. She had a wide forehead, rounded eyes, a perfectly straight nose, and rosy-coloured cheeks. There was nothing explicitly unpleasant about her looks, but she wasn't model material, not that I was model material either, mind you. Her face was softened by tendrils of hair that had escaped from her ponytail, and she had a wide and engaging smile, or at least she did when she was chatting to Ellie. Ellie was blessed with the power to put everyone at ease.

"Emma?" Tori interrupted my musings.

"What's that?"

"Don't 'what's that' me. I know you weren't listening. Come on, you can help me walk the dogs round the garden."

"I'd love to." I smiled at Tori. "I'm stuck here until Ellie's ready to leave anyway. She brought me."

"Great! I've got a surprise for you."

"For me?"

"Yep. Come on, this way."

We made our way to where those animals that were in for treatment were caged. I spotted my surprise immediately. "Angel!" I exclaimed. Angel belonged to one of my favourite clients, Mrs. Porter. She was an elderly lady who rescued anything furry. Angel was her latest. He was a ginormous black and tan Rottweiler with a perpetually slobbery grin.

"I thought he would put a smile on your face," Tori said, her own smile matching Angel's in size, although thankfully not in slobber.

"What's he in for?" I asked, unlatching his cage. Angel's stubby little tail was wagging so hard that I feared he was going to pull something.

"Nothing major, just some dental work. You take him, and I'll bring Lorenzo."

It didn't take long until we were outside in the practice garden. The sun shone overhead, making it a pleasant day for a wander, not that we were looking to walk far, not that we could have even if we'd wanted to. The 'garden' was really nothing more than a hundred-foot square-ish patch of land that had been fully secured. Its only purpose was to be somewhere for us to let the dogs have some fresh air (and a wee) before their owners collected them.

Tori and I chatted amiably while Angel and Lorenzo wandered about sniffing random blades of grass and doing what they needed to do.

"Brrr, it's getting cold," I commented. A noticeable breeze had risen, chilling me through.

"Is it?" Tori asked. She seemed undisturbed by the change in weather while I was finding it colder and colder.

"Maybe I've gotten soft after spending so long recuperating."

"Maybe, or maybe you were just a big ole softie all along," Tori teased.

"Ha ha," I said, shooting a look in her direction. The creepy thing was that while I was clearly in a draft, she wasn't. And neither were the dogs. With Angel, it was difficult to tell, his fur was akin to black velvet: smooth, sleek, and glossy. Lorenzo, however, was a white Pomeranian, complete with foxy-looking face, pointed ears, and mounds and mounds of fluffy white fur. Any kind of draft would have had a very obvious effect on his coat, but it wasn't moving, not even a little bit. A chill that had nothing to do with the weather slithered down my spine. "Now that really is weird," I muttered, more to myself than to Tori.

"What was that?" Tori asked.

"Nothing," I answered, unsure how to explain that a wind monster appeared to be after me. *Is that even a thing?* I wondered. Once upon a time I would have dismissed such ideas as utter nonsense, foolish flights of fantasy. But then I found out I was soulmates with the Grim Reaper and that my ancestors were keeping an eye on me. My nan's words came back to me in a flash. *Beware, Emma. Darkness surrounds you.* Between my first date with Blake and the fire that had followed, I was starting to get the sense that darkness really did surround me. I shivered, hoping that Ellie wouldn't be long.

Chapter 5 – Emma

Saturday 13ᵗʰ April 2019

A gust of wind threatened to topple me over as I struggled to get out of Ellie's car.

"Are you okay?" Ellie asked, already standing.

"Yes," I answered. "I just can't seem to find my feet because of the weather."

"But it's a beautiful day."

"Eh?" I asked, finally able to pull myself into a standing position. I looked at Ellie across the roof of her little Fiat 500 and immediately knew why I'd heard confusion in her voice. I was being battered by what felt like hurricane-level winds. Ellie on the other hand looked as though she'd been blessed by the gods of sunshine. She was standing in a beam of light that had broken through the puffy white clouds above. She looked like she was wearing a halo.

"What the . . ." I started to say, but a particularly vehement gust of wind stole the words from my mouth. I felt like I'd been dumped inside of a wind tunnel, not that I'd ever actually been inside one of those.

"We should get you inside," Ellie said. At least I think that's what she said. I could hardly hear her over the howling airstream.

I nodded my acquiescence and staggered towards my house. With Ellie's help, I was soon at the front door, where I was met with a particularly unpleasant sight.

My front door was an old wooden one that I'd painted a deep purple colour. Against its white frame, the solid block of colour usually popped. Except today it wasn't a solid block of colour, today it was smeared with streaks of dark red.

"What's that?" Ellie asked from behind me.

Barely able to breathe, let alone answer, I ignored Ellie in favour of unlocking the door. The key twisted easily in its lock, and I was soon able to step forwards into the porch. Out of the wind, I could finally catch my breath, and before looking too closely at the mess that had been left for me, I took a moment to fill my lungs. The scent of old pennies tickled my nose. "I have my suspicions," I answered.

"Well?" Ellie asked, still stood outside, no doubt enjoying the warming rays.

"I think it's blood," I answered, touching the door with my forefinger. Whatever the substance was, it felt tacky. It had been liberally daubed across the top of my door so that, as gravity had done what gravity does, streaks of it had run downwards. I lifted my hand up to my nose and sniffed . . . iron. It was definitely blood. "Yep," I concluded.

"You seem to be strangely okay about it," Ellie remarked, her eyebrow raised.

I laughed out loud. "Maybe I'm in shock?" I speculated, or maybe I simply couldn't take any more. Tidal waves of panic had lurked around every corner in recent weeks, threatening to drown me at any moment, but for some reason the presence of blood on my door didn't evoke a reaction. Maybe my mind was on the point of rupturing, so to protect itself, it'd finally built a dam.

"Why would someone do this?"

"I don't know, maybe Peter Collins had friends and they blame me for his death?"

"Maybe, but I think you should ring the police before we clean it off."

"I guess so. I'll ring Danny; he'll know what to do." Police Constable Danny Martin was the policeman who'd been assigned to my case when I'd first rung 111 to report the fact that I was being stalked. When he let his work mask slip, he seemed like a nice guy, and seeing as he'd left me his business card, I figured I may as well ring him direct. "Let me just check on the boys first," I finished. The boys were Cooper and Watson of course, my fur babies. Most people might say they were just cats. Most people would be wrong.

"Okay, but then you're ringing the police. I'll put the kettle on."

Cooper was already downstairs and happily followed Ellie into the kitchen, no doubt expecting sweeties. Turncoat! He was supposed to be my angel, not hers. Watson was nowhere to be seen, though, so I made my way upstairs, taking each step slowly and carefully. My ankle was definitely getting stronger, but I still had trust issues. While I'd hoped Watson would simply be lounging on one of the beds, expecting his people to come to him rather than the other way round, I actually found him underneath my bed in the front room.

"Watson's hiding," I said to Ellie a couple of minutes later. She was still making tea, so I joined her in the kitchen. "Something's definitely spooked him. He's sat hunched up underneath my bed. I guess whoever decorated my door frightened him."

"All of this is pretty strange, isn't it?" she remarked.

"Err, understatement of the year. First of all, my nan shoots me a warning, then there was the fire, and now I'm being attacked by a wind monster."

"And there's the blood on your door," Ellie added.

"And there's the blood," I agreed.

"Do you think they're all connected?"

"I don't know. I don't see how they can be, but I don't believe in coincidences of this magnitude."

"Me either." Ellie nodded thoughtfully. "Well, I wouldn't tell Danny about all of it," she concluded before placing my phone immediately in front of me in a not-so-subtle hint. It worked because I absentmindedly picked it up and started searching for Danny's card. "It's on the side of the boiler," Ellie helpfully supplied.

"Uh-huh," I responded, doing myself a disservice. My education was worth more than 'eh' or 'uh-huh.' "Dialling now." I keyed in Danny's phone number and hit the green button.

"It's Danny," he answered on the first ring.

"Hi Danny, it's Emma, Emma Moore, from when . . ."

"I remember," Danny interrupted.

"Phew!" I laughed nervously, wondering if everyone else felt an immediate surge of guilt whenever they spoke to a policeman. *How does his wife cope?* I wondered. "Something odd's happened, and I thought you might be able to advise." I paused, expecting some kind of response, but after an uncomfortable silence that might well have lasted for 89 years, 264 days, 13 hours and five seconds, I continued, "Someone's daubed blood on my front door. I figured I should be worried about it."

"You should," Danny replied brusquely. "I'll create an incident record and be out to see you in a while. Don't go anywhere." He paused briefly. "And Emma, weren't you also at The Sparrowhawk last night?"

"I was, but you can't possibly think that what happened there is in any way connected to this, can you? What happened at the pub was an accident, everyone says so."

"Hmmm, maybe, maybe not." I could picture him raising his eyebrows at me questioningly. We'd gotten to be on quite good terms in the aftermath of stalker-gate. I really hoped our 'relationship' hadn't withered on the vine in the past few weeks. Danny the professional was hugely intimidating, but Danny the real-live boy had a story of his own to tell. I'd just not worked out what it was yet.

I hung up and filled Ellie in. "Anyway, we may as well sit until he gets here," I finished, heading into the lounge and plonking myself down on one of the two sofas. "Unless you need to head off?" I asked.

"No, it's okay, I'll stay until Danny gets here." Ellie sat on the other sofa, which insinuated my house was palatial when really it wasn't. The lounge was just about big enough for two compact sofas to sit at right angles to each other. Both were positioned so that they were diagonally opposite the television, which stood on a slim oak dresser that was barely wide enough to house my digi-box and a handful of DVDs. Thank goodness for flat screen technology! I hadn't bothered with any other furniture in the lounge, apart from a lamp and a telephone point, but they didn't really count. My house was open-plan, and as a consequence, the lounge bled straight into the dining room. The archway between the two rooms took out most of the wall opposite the window and, with the stairway climbing a third wall, there simply wasn't space for anything else. "What are you going to tell your dad?"

I rolled my eyes, dreading that conversation. "How about nothing?" I asked hopefully.

"You need to tell him. Imagine how much worse it'll be if he finds out from someone else."

"You wouldn't!" I exclaimed, but Ellie said nothing, simply slumping back in her seat before sipping her tea. "Fine. But I'm not telling him it's blood."

I took Ellie's slight nod to be agreement, reached for my phone, and started texting. *Some idiot has graffitied my front door. Kids I expect. Anyway, I've called Danny and he's on his way out. I doubt he can do anything mind you. There's no need for you to come over, there's nothing you can do, Xx.* I didn't really believe children had been involved, but I hoped by laying the blame at an innocuous source, my dad wouldn't feel the need to worry or come over.

My phone chirruped fairly quickly alerting me of my dad's reply. *Okay. Love Dad.* And then it chirruped again. *Thank you for telling me.*

"He took that well," I remarked to Ellie.

"Let me guess, you downplayed it?"

"Well yeah. Just as you would have done if you'd had to tell your mum."

"I suppose," Ellie conceded. "Anyway, what are you going to wear to Charlotte's cocktail party on Friday?" Her face brightened from its usual 60-watt beam into a full 100-watt smile. Ellie *loved* both cocktails and parties. She'd been ecstatic with Charlotte's idea to host an event that combined two of her favourite things in one!

I pulled a face. "I was thinking about giving it a miss actually. You can go though," I quickly reassured.

"Nooo." Ellie drew out the 'o' as though seriously thinking about my statement. "That doesn't work for me," she concluded.

"But I don't want to go," I whined.

"I don't care."

"But . . ." I started to say, mentally scrambling for a reason as to why I shouldn't be forced to face Charlotte again.

"You're going, and that's the end of it. You owe Charlotte an apology anyway and this is the perfect opportunity for you to say you're sorry. Besides which, you need to start going out again."

"Urgh." I squirmed in my seat, wanting to argue against Ellie but also knowing that there was no real point. Ellie always won these kinds of arguments. Mostly she was sunshine and light, but once she'd decided on something, there was absolutely no moving her. She was a solid block of concrete that had been reinforced with steel girders. The worst of it was that she always won with a smile on her face and she never raised her voice, she just stood firm. "Fine," I muttered.

"So, what are you wearing then?" Ellie smiled, safe in the knowledge that I'd be wearing whatever she thought was most suitable.

"Jeans and a T-shirt?" I asked hopefully.

"Charlotte specifically asked us to dress up."

"Okay, I'll give it some thought."

Satisfied, Ellie changed the subject. "So, what did you and Blake talk about last night? You haven't told me yet."

"Everything and nothing," I replied before relaying—almost word for word—my dinner conversation from the night before. We were both laughing at Blake's first taste of wine when a knock on the window startled me. The smile slid from my face and my heart jumped into my throat, constricting my windpipe and making it hard to breathe.

"It's just Danny," Ellie said reassuringly, getting up to let him in. "You scared her, she'll just be a second," I heard her explain quietly to him. I didn't catch his reply, but I did hear her answer, "No, she's fine, she's been avoiding excursions ever since, well . . . you know. And loud noises make her jump now, but who can blame her after what she's been through," she finished.

"I'm fine," I declared, standing. I wasn't fine actually, my legs were a little on the shaky side, but I didn't feel as though I had any right to be afraid. It was over, I'd won, I'd survived. Why did the old nervous system keep kicking in at the most inopportune moments? "I'm fine," I said again, reiterating the point more for my own benefit rather than anyone else's. "Come in, Danny, hi. Why did you knock on the window?" I asked.

"The blood," he explained, joining me in the lounge but not sitting. "I didn't want to touch it. I've taken pictures and spoken to your neighbours. No one had anything concrete to report, but one of the older ladies across the road said she saw a couple of smartly dressed men knocking about earlier. She didn't pay much attention to them because of how they were dressed, so she can't say anything for sure other than the fact they were definitely men and they were definitely suited. She can't even say if they lingered long enough to have done that to your door." Danny pointed at 'that' to reiterate his point.

"Great." I sighed. "So in the nicest possible way, you've got nothing."

"Correct," Danny concluded, his hands now loosely clasped in front of his body. "But I did open an incident for you, and I will keep it marked as under investigation for the next few weeks. If anything else happens, ring me straight away."

"Of course, who else would I ring?"

The corners of Danny's mouth lifted slightly at my rhetorical question, hinting at the fact that there was more to him than just the snippets he showed. "I see your cast is off," he remarked.

"Yep. I got given the all-clear yesterday. I'm officially allowed to do stuff again."

"Good, I seem to recall telling you to move on with your life."

"You did. And I will."

"This isn't what I had in mind." He raised an eyebrow suggestively, but I was left unsure of his meaning.

"As you well know, I went out last night," I argued, my natural sarcastic tendencies reasserting themselves.

"That's more like it." Danny smiled wryly. Had he pushed me on purpose? "Anyway, you might as well clean up now."

"What? You're not going to send round some lab techs?" Ellie interrupted.

Danny shook his head ever so slightly. "Nope, they won't be able to tell you anything other than it's blood, and we know that already."

"Couldn't you get some DNA from it?"

"I doubt it. It's probably pig's blood. Maybe lambs. I highly doubt it's human."

"What about fingerprints?" I asked hopefully. I'd seen plenty of crime shows over the years.

"Whoever did this to your door didn't even touch it. You can see the brush marks if you look closely. Someone created a work of art for you to find."

"Did they?" I asked, pushing past Danny and yanking open the front door to inspect it again. *Huh, Danny was right,* I thought to myself. When I peered at it, I could just about see what he'd been referring to. In fact, when I squinted, I realised that someone had actually drawn a symbol on my door. It had been mostly obscured by the drips, but it sort of looked like three horizontal lines stacked neatly on top of each other. They all seemed to be around about the same length and width, although I couldn't tell whether that had been done on purpose or not. The middle one, though, was more of a zig-zag instead of a straight line. "How bizarre," I remarked to no one in particular.

"Indeed. I'll do a search when I get back to the station for similar incidents. Maybe this is gang related?" Danny stepped past me and out of the house. Without thinking, I followed, and the wind from earlier struck again, bypassing Danny but tugging forcefully at my clothes.

"That's strange," Danny commented, unconsciously reaching up to brush his hair off his face, even though he was not affected by the wind; not a single strand of his hair was out of place.

"You know what they say about March winds," I laughed lamely, hurrying back inside.

"Emma, it's April."

"Well, yes, but perhaps they're running late. Anyway, thanks for everything." I quickly shut the front door in his face and breathed a sigh of relief. No doubt Danny now thought I was rude, and maybe a little on the odd side, but how could I explain something that I didn't understand myself? "He's gone," I said to Ellie, but she'd gone too.

"In here," she called from the kitchen. "Seeing as you seem to be legitimately trapped in your house by the mysterious winds, I figured I'd best clean up." She emerged with a bucket filled with soapy water and a sponge.

Chapter 6 – Blake

Saturday 13th April 2019

Blake meandered through Joanne and Frank's house at a leisurely pace, completely at ease, without any sense of wrongdoing. He'd spent almost a thousand years watching people, and as a consequence, it never occurred to him that what he was doing was snooping. He was simply curious about the souls of Ellie and her mum, Joanne.

Blake had lived a mostly incorporeal life, unseen by all except those on their deathbeds, those remnants that remained behind after death, and Seith. That had only changed when he'd met Emma, but she had to be close by for her bubble to affect him. Therefore he knew that he was essentially invisible.

Joanne and Frank's house was a large detached dwelling built in its own grounds on the edge of a small village. When Blake had first entered it, he'd found himself in a formal sitting room, decorated mostly in grey: grey carpet, grey wallpaper, and a grey suite. The only splash of colour was to be found on a feature wall, which was a dark blue at the bottom but faded to a pure white at the top. Blake approved.

At the back of the room, glass doors separated the lounge from the kitchen-come-diner, which ran across the back of the house. The glass barrier would have proved an obstacle for some but not Blake, between one stride and the next, he simply passed through it. Even knowing what it might have felt like, he felt absolutely nothing, not even a hint of resistance.

He found himself in the kitchen half of the back room first. It was decorated in neutral tones, the cupboards (and the matching island unit) were cream with a dark wooden countertop, the flooring was the same dark wood, and the walls were magnolia. Joanne stood at the island unit mixing what he thought was cream cheese frosting for a cake, and so he loitered to watch her work. If only he could taste and smell in his usual state of existence. He reached out to dip a finger into the yellowy-looking goo, but of course his finger came away clean, and he sighed in frustration.

In the dining half of the room, a dark wooden table that matched the countertop sat in front of a second set of glass doors. Passing through them, Blake popped out in a utility room, decorated in much the same way as the kitchen-diner. For most people there was only one way in and one way out of the utility room, but Blake was not most people. He pushed on through the wall until he found himself in a study. This room was decorated in different shades of green; Joanne and Frank were obviously not afraid of colour. The carpet was the darkest block of colour; it looked as though it would be plush and comfortable underfoot, but Blake could only guess at what it would feel like to walk upon. In stark comparison to the carpet, the walls were so pale that they were almost colourless. Oak shelving, filled with books and the occasional ornament, ran along the entirety of one wall, and a solid oak desk (upon which stood a fairly standard desk lamp) sat in the centre of the room.

Blake paused for a moment, sitting on the chair that accompanied the desk. Of course, he didn't actually sit, his bottom didn't really make contact with the chair, but he appeared to be seated, to himself anyway. He found himself looking out of the window at a spectacular view, mile upon mile of greenery. Joanne and Frank lived in a nice part of the British countryside.

Although the view was lovely to look at, it didn't provide Blake with any answers. With nothing more than a thought, he relocated himself to the first floor. The layout was much the same as the downstairs, with Ellie's bedroom above the lounge and her parents' above the kitchen-diner. He'd wandered throughout the whole of the upstairs when he heard the front door slam.

"Mum?" Ellie called.

"In here," Joanne replied.

Blake stilled to listen in on their conversation.

"How was Emma?" Joanne continued.

"Yeah, she's fine. Still freaking out but telling everyone she's okay," Ellie answered. It sounded as though she was moving through the house and into the kitchen, where her mum still stood baking. "Mmm, what are you cooking?"

"A chocolate and orange cake. You can take some to Emma and her new boyfriend tomorrow. In fact, I might come with you. I'd like to get to know Blake a little better myself. And maybe I can get her to open up about what she's going through."

"You can try, but she'll just tell you she's fine. She's doing her best ostrich impression."

Blake considered joining them when he heard his name mentioned but decided against it, preferring to remain where he was. Joanne's voice had had a definite edge in it when she'd said his name.

"It smells good in here. Where's Dad?" Ellie asked.

"He's still at work; he'll be home soon. So, how did you get on at Cedar's?"

"Good actually. Emma reckons she'll be back at work next week. I'm not so sure she'll manage it."

"She just needs a bit of time."

"Hmmm, maybe."

"Did something else happen today? Something unusual?"

"Not really. Well . . . I suppose so. Emma's front door was vandalised. Someone painted blood on it, although we haven't told her parents that bit. You know how freaked out Ian would be if he found out. Creepy hey? Who do you think would do something like that?"

Despite how he currently felt about Emma, Blake very nearly left when he heard Ellie say that blood had been daubed on her front door. He felt an urge to check on her, to reassure himself that she was okay. However, intrigue got the better of him and he stayed still.

"Who indeed?" Joanne answered, a strange catch in her voice. "Did Emma cope okay?"

"With the door, yes, but not when Danny arrived. He knocked on the window, making her jump."

"Poor girl, she's been through so much."

"She has. I still don't understand why she's trying to hide her fears though. After everything she's been through, she's entitled to be a little freaked out, and she knows she can talk to me about anything."

"I don't think she's doing it consciously. I don't think she's hiding her feelings from you as such, I think she's hiding them from herself. She doesn't want to admit that she's still struggling. Or maybe she thinks that if she doesn't acknowledge her fears, they aren't real."

There was a brief pause, and then Ellie replied, "Maybe."

Joanne's words had given Blake pause for thought as well. He still struggled with the vast welter of human emotion. Yes, what Peter Collins had done had been horrible; Blake himself had intervened because he hadn't been able to bear the idea of any harm coming to Emma, but it was over. Why did she have to keep revisiting the memories? Why couldn't she just let it go? He'd repeatedly reassured her that she was in no danger of dying any time soon, and he would know, he was drawn to death in much the same way as a moth was drawn to a flame. He could easily sense when someone's life hung in the balance, and hers didn't. It baffled Blake that Emma didn't trust his word on the matter.

Lost in thought as he was, Blake missed the end of the conversation between Ellie and Joanne. His ears only pricked up again when Ellie burst into her own bedroom to find an unexpected guest.

Chapter 7 – Ellie

Saturday 13ᵗʰ April 2019

Scott lounged comfortably on Ellie's bed, his legs crossed at the ankle and his hands behind his head. He'd had the good grace to kick off his work shoes before putting his feet up, but he'd left them strewn where they'd fallen. Equally his work jacket lay on the floor where it had been dumped.

"Why hellooo, my daaarling," he drawled before Ellie had time to say anything.

"Scott! What are you—? Why are you—? What's with the dumbass accent?" Ellie might have only just started to acknowledge that what she felt for Scott was love, but that hadn't stopped her from dreaming about finding him in her bedroom before, preferably naked and dipped in melted chocolate. He was after all a fine specimen of a man. "Does my mum know you're up here?" she asked.

"What's wrong with my accent?" Scott sat in one fluid movement and thrust his bottom lip out so far that he could only have been pouting, but Ellie didn't think she'd ever seen Scott pout. Emma, yes; there was no denying that Emma was a sulker. When she didn't get her own way, it was best just to leave her to own devices until she'd thrown off the funk. But Scott . . . he was different. He was good-humoured, kind, and gentle. Not that Emma wasn't kind or gentle, but she was more reserved. She was incredibly loyal to those she held dear, but people had to earn her trust. Scott was more laidback, more like Ellie. Other than baiting his sister (which he did often and just for the fun of it), there wasn't a bad bone in his body.

"Scott, seriously! What are you doing here?" Ellie asked, shutting the door behind her and dropping her bag in the corner before turning to face him properly.

"Not Scott," Scott replied, all trace of the fake accent gone.

"What do you mean 'not Scott'?" An edge crept into Ellie's voice as she became increasingly frustrated. "We grew up together. I've been watching everything you do for over twenty years. Don't you think I'd recognise you?"

"Not Scott. We didn't grow up together. And you've been watching me?"

"Honestly, Scott, if you only came over to play stupid games you may as well go."

"Huh," Scott said, a quizzical look crossing his face. "I thought you'd find the Scott suit more agreeable than anything else. Maybe not."

"Scott!" Ellie all but yelled at him, stamping her foot and clenching her hands tightly into fists.

"How about this one?" Scott asked, standing and turning in a circle. By the time he was facing Ellie again, it wasn't Scott that stood in front of her, it was Matthew, complete with piercing blue eyes and sandy blonde hair.

"Matthew!" Ellie gasped. "How did you—? What's going on here?"

"Not Matthew either," Scott-Matthew said.

"Scott! Matthew! Whoever the hell you are! What are you doing in my bedroom?" Ellie demanded.

"Awww, don't be like that," Scott-Matthew whined. "This is such a fun game. Hey, what about if I try on a female face?" he said, turning again. Ellie watched in disbelief, unable to look away, as Matthew transformed in front of her eyes. His frame shifted from the lean, slight one of Matthew into the petite, dumpy one of Charlotte, complete with full bust, rounded stomach, and ample derriere. His hair changed from a sandy blonde colour, growing longer and darker by the second; his lips became fuller and his eyes darkened. Even his skin tone altered, taking on the ruddy complexion that Ellie associated with Charlotte.

"Wha—" Ellie started to say but was interrupted by the Scott-Matthew-Charlotte-whoever-whatever person-thing who'd broken into her room.

"Ooh, one more please," Charlotte begged, literally clasping her hands together in prayer and bending at the knees. "Pleeeaaassseee, it's such a good one." She turned quickly without giving Ellie time to argue. "Well?" Emma asked a moment later.

"Emma," Ellie gasped. "Is it really you? Can you change your look now? That's creepy." She shuddered in distaste.

"Seriously?" Emma drawled. "You actually think I'm Emma?"

"Erm, if you're not Emma, who the hell are you?"

"Why, I'm Abaddon of course, here to bestow you with the angelic gifts you'll need for the forthcoming battle. Haven't you been expecting me?"

"No. Funnily enough I haven't been expecting you because I haven't been expecting anyone to arbitrarily break into my house. Now for the last time, who are you, what the hell are you doing in my room, and how in God's name do you keep changing into different people?"

"Huh, you really don't know me, do you?" Abaddon looked genuinely baffled as she plopped back onto the bed, still wearing Emma's face.

"Oh my God no, I really don't know you."

"Well, I have to say, I'm impressed you're not more freaked out then."

Ellie sighed. "My best friend is soulmates with the Grim Reaper; I'm starting to expect the unexpected. And remind me again why I'm explaining this to you and not just kicking you out."

"It's one of my angelic powers," Abaddon answered, looking Ellie straight in the eye.

"Angelic powers?"

"Yep, I engender trust. People can't help but warm to me. They feel compelled to overshare. It can be a bit of a pain in the backside, to be honest; sometimes I just want a yes-no answer and I'll get *War and Peace*, or I'll be ordering a latte and the barista feels like they have to tell me every single health violation that the coffee shop has ever made. Some people become waaay too talkative, others just let little nuggets slip, like you. Urgh, it's so . . ."

"Can you stop for a minute and back up?" Ellie interrupted. "You're an angel? What makes you think I should know you?"

"You're the Guardian, aren't you? I mean, you know all about the Keeper of Souls, don't you?"

"In so much as I recently found out my best friend has inherited a portion of his soul from her ancestors and is now sleeping with him, yes, I know all about Blake. How is that relevant? And can't you switch off whatever it is that's making me tell you everything?"

"She's sleeping with him!" Abaddon exclaimed gleefully, ignoring everything else that Ellie had said. Ellie felt a little disorientated watching Abaddon, who looked exactly like Emma, bounce up and down excitedly like a little child. Emma never behaved with such gay abandon. "That is sooo juicy. None of us foresaw that happening. Although I suppose we should have done. Everyone who's ever carried the soul before Emma has been drawn to Blake, they've just never quite connected before. Really, It was only a matter of time until the two halves of the golden soul were reunited. We all thought it would have happened long before now, to be honest."

"Who's we?"

"Come on, you must know who I am. You have been told about your heritage, haven't you? Joanne's going to get a right royal ass-kicking if she hasn't clued you in."

"What has my mum got to do with this? She doesn't even know who Blake is."

"Ha! That's where you're wrong. Your mum knows exactly who he is. She's very clear on her destiny. And she should have told you about yours. In fact, I think I'll go and have it out with her right now." Abaddon stood swiftly and brushed past Ellie as she reached for the door.

"Wait!" Ellie really didn't want to get her mum involved in any of what was going on. "Why don't you tell me what's going on? Frankly, my mum will just muddy the waters and overcomplicate things. And please, can you change your look again?" Ellie sat on the vanity stool, hoping that if she stayed put, Abaddon would as well.

"But I like being the Key." Abaddon's face fell. "She's so pretty."

"The Key? What does that mean? And if you're talking about Emma, I agree, she *is* pretty, but she doesn't see herself that way. She'd probably tell you that she's too tall, too fat or both."

"But she's got a banging body. I'm already thinking about taking it for a proper joyride. Ooh, the things I'm going to do in it," Abaddon said, her face brightening at whatever it was she'd just decided to do.

"I'm sure you're just as pretty."

"Well, d'oh. Of course I am, but my true form is a little showy for you mere mortals."

"So, erm . . . can I see it then?"

"Sneaky!" Abaddon clapped in delight. "I see what you just did then. You're going to make an awesome Guardian." She nodded in agreement with herself. "Are you sure about this?"

Ellie tilted her head in response.

"Okay then," Abaddon agreed, turning slowly in a circle. The transformation was the most dramatic yet. Abaddon, when not 'dressed' as a character, stood approximately seven feet tall. She was slim but not overly so; instead her muscular body formed the perfect hourglass. She had long white-blonde hair that had been plaited into a single braid and pulled forward over her left shoulder, where it hung down to her waist. Her eyes gleamed bright blue. To Ellie, they looked almost radioactive, such was the glow that emanated from them. Her skin was the colour of china, but her lips were fuchsia pink. And her wings! They looked like pearlescent glass, glossy and smooth. "Oh, I almost forgot, one more thing." Abaddon snapped her fingers and immediately a blinding white light filled the room, forcing Ellie to look down and cover her eyes. "Too much?" Abaddon asked.

"My eyes," Ellie replied, unable to look up, but almost before she'd finished speaking, the light flared and then dimmed.

When Ellie was finally able to see again, Abaddon stood proudly in front of her, her wings tucked out of sight. "What do you think of my outfit?" she asked, twisting first to the left and then to the right.

"It's a bit obvious," Ellie remarked, not even trying to sugarcoat her opinion. Abaddon was dressed from head-to-toe in white leather: strappy stiletto sandals with four-inch heels were laced up over her ankles, hot pants dipped low at her waist, and a tightly fitted bustier just about covered her upper assets, leaving her midriff and arms completely bare.

"Do you think?" Abaddon looked down at herself. "Maybe," she concluded, giving herself a little shake to change her outfit. The only thing that changed, though, was the colour. White was replaced with a shade of pink that closely matched her lips. "There," she declared. "So, what do you want to know?" she finished, sitting on the edge of Ellie's bed and crossing one leg over the other.

"How do you walk in those things?" Ellie blurted, obviously still affected by Abaddon's peculiar power, because while that was her first thought, it wasn't the most sensible of questions.

"These?" Abaddon gently jiggled her foot, clearly indicating her shoes. "Oh, I don't walk in these. I only ever wear them when I'm not walking anywhere. Maybe when I'm on a date, play-acting at being nothing more than a lowly little human. I can just about totter into a restaurant with them on. I couldn't go dancing in them or anything like that. They're so cute, though, aren't they? Anyway, that isn't what you wanted to know, is it? What do you really want to know?"

"Everything, I guess. Who are you? I mean, not just your name, but who are you? Why do you think I'm the Guardian, the Guardian of what? And what has my mum got to do with any of this?"

"Seriously, Joanne has been slacking in her duties if you're this ignorant," she said, glaring at Ellie.

"Hey! I'm not ignorant."

"Uh-huh, if you say so." Abaddon pulled a face that very clearly said she didn't agree with Ellie despite what she'd said. "Now, where do I start . . . ."

"How about at the beginning?"

"That would make for a very long and very boring story. The beginning happened many, many millennia ago and, to be honest, not much happened in the early days. It took God several years to even realise he'd woken up and was conscious, and after that it took him many more years to design and build the three dimensions."

"The three dimensions?" Ellie asked.

"Yes, Heaven, Hell, and the in-between dimension. Now, stop interrupting, otherwise this will take all day." Abaddon paused, gathering her thoughts, and then began a moment later. "Your story starts around about the same time as Emma's. Please tell me you know her origins because the whole John-Bronwyn thing is far too urgh for me. Good," she said, noting that Ellie had nodded. "When John was the Keeper of Souls, he had more than one purpose. Yes, he reaped the souls of the dying, thus safeguarding the energy of creation. I assume you know that much despite your limited understanding, but what you probably don't know is that John's primary function was to operate as a portal between the dimensions."

"A portal?" Ellie interrupted despite Abaddon's instruction not to.

Abaddon paused, glaring coldly at Ellie before continuing. "When he did what he did—"

"Wait! When who did what?" Ellie asked, earning herself another dark look. Abaddon the angel was not all that angelic!

"When John committed suicide," Abaddon continued through gritted teeth. Privately, Ellie thought that was an unpleasant way of putting it, but she held her tongue. " . . . he effectively closed the door between the realms. Those angels and demons who were here were trapped here, and those who were in Heaven or Hell were trapped there, unable to join their brothers and sisters here. As you know, after John's death, Blake came into being. He continued to reap the souls of the dying in much the same way that John did. However, he's never been able to function as a portal. Only when the whole soul is back together again will Blake be able to fulfil all of his duties and give us access to all three dimensions."

"This . . . it just doesn't sound believable," Ellie scoffed.

"What? You can accept the Keeper of Souls is real but not this? It's not like I've just told you that Santa Claus is real, and that he really does deliver the presents on Christmas Eve night, although it would be cool if he did. I wouldn't mind a ride on his sleigh." Abaddon smirked.

"Okay, but I don't get it. What's my role in all of this? I'm the Guardian of what?"

"Ah, that! There are those who want to use Blake for their own nefarious means. To do that, they need Emma because she's the Key. That's where you come in. You're her Guardian."

"So I have to, what, keep Emma safe or keep her away from Blake?"

"Not exactly. Your job is to keep the portal from opening any which way you can. The only way I can think of doing that is to kill Emma. She's the Key after all, without her—"

"WHAT?!" Ellie cut Abaddon off. "There's no way I'm killing anyone and especially not Emma; she's my best friend."

"Then your world will be overwhelmed by demons when they get hold of Emma and perform the ritual," Abaddon stated plainly.

"Demons?"

"Weren't you listening? Demons do exist."

"But kill Emma? That's not happening. Why don't we just explain the situation to her and ask her to stay away from Blake."

"It's too late for that. There are plenty of people who know who she is, and now that she's met Blake, they can force her to act."

"Couldn't they have done that anyway?"

"No, thankfully that's always been a bit of a failsafe. The Key had to meet Blake in order to be able to call for him."

"Well, I'm not killing her; there must be another option. There must be something else we can do, something else we can try," Ellie implored.

"Such as?" While Ellie's mind struggled to grasp everything Abaddon had said, Abaddon busied herself by polishing her nails, using Ellie's bedspread to buff them, and then, with a flick of her fingers, they changed from au natural to white and then to black before settling on a 'dipped' look, black at the cuticle and white at the tip.

"Wait! Wait!" Ellie declared. "Why doesn't Blake just not open the portal?"

"You really think it's that easy?"

"Isn't it?"

"No."

"Why not?"

Abaddon sighed loudly, rolling her eyes. "Joanne deserves the biggest ass-kicking ever for not filling you in." She shook her head in dismay but did go on to explain, "John had centuries to learn how to be the portal before God even thought about creating Earth here in the in-between. He wasn't just a door; he was also a gatekeeper. In the time of angels and demons, when this realm was nothing more than a vacuous space, John learned how to control his gift. By the time Earth was conjured into being by the almighty, John's will was absolute; nothing got between the dimensions unless he explicitly allowed it. In comparison, Blake will be like a child playing with a nuclear reactor."

"But," Ellie argued, "maybe the demons aren't all that bad?"

"Oh, they're bad. The ones here already are evidence enough of that. You have to remember that angels and demons are extremes, opposite ends of the spectrum: good-evil, light-dark, white-black. The demons are really bad."

"You don't seem all that good to me," Ellie muttered under her breath.

"I heard that," Abaddon remarked. "Just because I like to have a little fun, it doesn't mean that I'm not inherently good. Ultimately I want what's best for all three dimensions. The demons don't care about anything other than what they want."

"Fine. Maybe they just won't come."

"Seriously! You have been given a brain, you know. You should use it once in a while. The demons will come. Heck, even the angels will come. Only in the in-between is there any colour, that's why angels and demons fought so hard for control of it before God created you lot and let you guys have it."

"You fought?"

"All the time. We had huge epic battles almost every other week. God could have stepped in at any time, but he never did. He was all blah-blah-blah you're old enough to know better, blah-blah-blah learn how to share."

"Why didn't John keep you all in your own dimensions then?"

"I don't know. Maybe he enjoyed the battles. He only really started exerting his will when he met Bronwyn."

"What about God though? Surely he'd save us?"

"Didn't you hear what I just said? You kiddies may be younger than we are, but he's as bored of you as he is of us. Your only option is to kill Emma, although I have to admit it's not the best plan. All we'll really be doing is kicking the can down the road because the soul will be reborn in time." Abaddon stood, stretched, and started pacing.

Ellie's bedroom was roughly the same size as Emma's house; Abaddon had plenty of space. It was decorated in shades of yellow. The walls were a pale lemony colour, while the curtains, bedspread, and various scatter cushions were a dark amber adorned with sunflowers. Abaddon paced backwards and forwards, pausing mid-way through her first circuit of the room to shake each of her feet in turn. The stilettos were replaced with much more sensible fluffy bunny slippers. Ellie just watched, holding her breath, letting everything that Abaddon had said sink in and hoping that she would come up with a solution that was more palatable than the one she'd been offered so far. Not that she had any intention of killing Emma anyway. But she wasn't so keen on the idea of fighting in a war against demons either.

"Maybe what we need is a cleaving," Abaddon muttered, stopping suddenly and tapping her newly polished nails on her lip.

"How does that help?"

Abaddon looked at Ellie quizzically. "Given the lack of your education, what do you actually know about souls?"

"Not much, I guess. We all have one."

"That's not exactly true. Humans have them. Angels and demons do not." Abaddon took a deep breath and continued, "Souls are a gift from God. They are quite literally the energy of creation. That's why Blake reaps them; they're too powerful for others to get their grubby little mitts on. Once he's reaped a soul, it remains inside him until such time that a child of the same lineage is born. Blake probably doesn't even know he's doing it, but essentially he stores the souls and then passes them along when the time is right."

Ellie raised her hand, speaking only when Abaddon paused for breath. "What if a child of the same lineage is never born?"

"You're thinking about this too literally. It isn't a simple case of parent to child; you need to factor in aunts, uncles, cousins, the whole of the family."

"Fine, but the population is growing," Ellie pointed out.

"Good point, but so too is the number of souls. Between bodies, they fracture and split in two before swelling to the right size. The only one that's never done that is the golden soul, Blake and Emma's."

"Uh-huh."

"Now then, the only time a soul is not recycled is when it is cleaved apart with the scythe. Then the soul ceases to exist. The energy dissipates into the ether, evaporating into nothing. If we do that to Emma's half of the soul, then it can't be re-joined with Blake's. That's it! That's what we'll have to do." Abaddon clapped her hands together with glee and did a little jig.

"Wait!" Ellie held up her hands. "Your plan still requires Emma to die."

"Well, yes, that's a given."

"No, it's not happening. Guardians guard, so that's what I'll do. I'll protect Emma from harm."

"Guardians guard! Have you heard yourself?" Abaddon scoffed. "Guardians make sure their prisoners do not bring about the end of the world. Your destiny is to watch Emma and make sure she does not enable Blake to open the portal."

"No, give your angelic gifts to someone else. I'll stand by Emma until the end if I have to."

"Don't be silly. You're the one who's prophesied to receive the gifts."

"There's a prophecy?"

"There's always a prophecy. And it says you're it. You're the one with angel blood in your veins."

"I don't have angel blood in my veins," Ellie exclaimed.

"Of course you do, how else could your body absorb my gifts? I injected my own blood into your great-great-great, wait . . . how many greats should there be now? Well whatever, I injected my own blood into her womb so that it was absorbed into your great-great-add-in-any-number-of-greats-grandfather. Your name has been foretold since that very day, Eleanor Chapman-Bell."

"No! Go to hell; this isn't happening." Ellie stood in the heat of the moment, challenging Abaddon, not that Abaddon appeared even the slightest bit bothered.

"This," Abaddon waved her hand indicating all of Ellie, "this right here is why Joanne is now going to get an ass-kicking. You were never meant to grow up alongside the Key. You were never meant to be friends with her. You should, however, have been trained and prepared. You . . ." she pointed her perfectly manicured nail at Ellie, "stay here, and you . . ." She turned and pointed towards the seemingly empty corner of the room. "It's nice to see you again, Blakey. Now you know."

Abaddon's last words chilled Ellie through.

Chapter 8 – Ellie

Saturday 13th April 2019

"Mum!" Ellie yelled, jogging down the stairs at pace, ignoring Abaddon's instruction to 'stay.' "Mum!" She burst into the kitchen, not entirely sure what she was expecting, but it certainly wasn't Joanne hugging Abaddon tightly into her. "Mum," she gasped.

Joanne and Abaddon broke apart. They looked so different that Ellie nearly laughed out loud. Joanne was petite with short, bobbed, blonde hair. She was dressed comfortably in jeans and an old woollen jumper that was so faded it could only be described as grey. Abaddon, in comparison, was still in her true form. She towered above Joanne and, other than the fluffy bunny slippers, was still dressed like a hooker.

"Oh yeah," Abaddon drawled. "So, there's something I want to talk to you about." She arched her eyebrows at Joanne, an edge creeping into her voice. "And you," she pointed at Ellie, "I told you to stay upstairs."

"As if that was going to happen," Ellie huffed.

"What . . ." Joanne started to say but her voice trailed off. She looked between Ellie and Abaddon. "You've told her, haven't you?"

"You should have told her," Abaddon stated, poking Joanne in the chest.

"It's true?" Ellie asked at the same time. "Why didn't you tell me?"

Joanne's shoulders sagged. "I wanted you to have a normal life. I didn't want you involved in any of this."

"That's so messed up. Does Dad know?"

"No." Joanne shook her head. "He doesn't know anything about any of this."

"Grammy knew, though, didn't she?" Ellie's brain was working quickly now, putting little snippets of information that she'd heard over the years together. "Does this, whatever it is, come from her?"

"Yes, Grammy knew, but no, it doesn't come from her. Our duty was passed down to us from Grandpa Harold."

Ellie's eyes widened in amazement. "I think I need a drink," she said, heading for the sideboard where the spirits were kept.

"Ellie!" Joanne gasped, switching into mummy-mode even though Ellie was nearer to thirty than she was to twenty.

"What? Don't you need a drink?" Ellie asked over her shoulder.

"Ooh, let's have mojitos," Abaddon chipped in, emphasising her words with a little salsa dance. As she gyrated her hips, turning in a full circle, she transformed again. By the time she faced Ellie, her height was more normal and, instead of the alabaster complexion, her skin was the colour of milky coffee. Her eyes glittered darkly in their sockets, and her raven-coloured hair was tied in a top-knot. In her hands she held a circular tray on which stood three tall glasses, each filled to the brim with crushed ice, fresh sprigs of mint, wedges of lime, and what Ellie assumed was rum.

As Ellie stepped forwards to reach for one of the glasses, Joanne surprised her by saying, "Just gin for me, but make it a strong one," before lapsing into an awkward silence, which hung heavily in the air.

It was Abaddon that broke it. "I haven't got all day, y'all." She slipped easily into the accent that Ellie had first heard her use. "Things to do, places to go, people to do. Oopsy, I mean people to see." She laughed wickedly, winking at Ellie. "Are we doing this here, stood up in the kitchen where all the best paaar-taaays happen? Or shall we retire to the dining table for a civilised discussion? And seriously, Joanne, when are you going to offer me a piece of that cake I can see?"

It was almost impossible not to laugh at just how outrageous and extravagant Abaddon was. Both Ellie and Joanne found themselves smiling, and without further prompting, Joanne retrieved the newly baked, freshly iced, chocolate orange sponge while Ellie fetched crockery and cutlery.

When they were all seated—Abaddon at the head of the table with Joanne and Ellie at either side—Joanne spoke up. "I guess I owe you an explanation," she said to Ellie, before sipping on her drink, which, as requested, had been replaced by a gin, complete with the classic fishbowl glass.

"I guess so," Ellie agreed. "How could you keep all of this from me for all these years? From Dad? What is all of this anyway? Am I really the Guardian? Is Emma really the Key? Do you really know who Blake is?" The questions poured from Ellie like water from an open tap.

"Blimey, that's a lot of questions." Joanne forked cake into her mouth, chewed, swallowed, and then answered, "Believe it or not, it was easy to keep it from you and Dad, yes, yes, and yes. Well, I've suspected who he was for a while now, but I wasn't sure. I take it he really is the Keeper of Souls?"

Ellie nodded but didn't answer.

"Ellie, you need to let me explain things properly."

"Go on then, explain away. Explain how you could lie to me for all of these years." A hard edge had crept into Ellie's voice, one that even she was surprised to hear.

"I never lied to you, Ellie. I just didn't tell you everything."

"A lie of omission is still a lie, Mum."

"Ellie, please. You've never spoken to me like this before."

"I've never known you to keep secrets from me before."

"If I may," Abaddon interjected. "Please don't forget that you're both still affected by my angelic power. As you may recall, I engender trust. People feel compelled to overshare, that is, they can't help but be honest."

Ellie took a deep breath in, releasing it slowly and purposely before speaking again, "I'm sorry, Mum, I shouldn't have spoken to you like that, but you have to admit this is a lot for me to take on board."

"No, I'm sorry." Joanne shook her head slightly. "I should have said something sooner, but I just . . . I don't know . . . I spent my entire childhood terrified that a demon was about to attack. Grandpa Harold told me everything when I was only five. From that day on, I lived in fear, and it wasn't like I could talk to anyone about why I was afraid. I just . . . I didn't want that for you."

Ellie leant across the table and took her mum's hand in her own. "Why did Grandpa Harold tell you when you were so young?"

"Because his dad didn't tell him until he was older. He always said it was like a bombshell being dropped on him. I guess I made his mistake, huh?"

"I don't suppose there's a right or a wrong answer in these circumstances, is there?"

"If there is, I don't know it."

Ellie sat up straight again and took a swig of her drink. It tasted sweet and refreshing but the rum burned the back of her throat. Apparently Abaddon liked her cocktails strong. "Why don't you just start at the beginning?"

"Okay, the beginning," Joanne started before pausing to collect her thoughts. "As I said, I was five when Grandpa Harold sat me down and told me that he had a secret to share with me. He said I was old enough to understand and that he was trusting me not to tell anyone else, not even your Uncle Clark or your Uncle Dale."

"Don't they know?" Ellie asked, surprised to hear the names of her uncles because they weren't a close family. If it hadn't been for Grammy's funeral, it would have been years since she'd even seen them.

"No, they don't know. Or at least, I've never told them anything. Part of the reason I keep them at arm's length is so that I don't let anything slip. Well, that and the fact that they are quite a bit older than I am."

"So what did Grandpa Harold say?"

"You know most of it, he told me about the love affair between John and Bronwyn. He told me what John did, and then he told me that one of his ancestors had been visited by an angel."

"That was me," Abaddon squealed with delight, clapping her hands together with glee.

"Yes, that was you," Joanne replied, smiling kindly at her. "Abaddon here told Hilde what had happened and that the child needed a Guardian, someone who would watch over her and take action if required."

"By take action . . .?" Ellie asked, allowing her voice to trail off.

"Yes, Ellie, I mean that I've always known there was a chance I would have to kill Emma. If that's what's needed to stop the apocalypse, then that's what I'll do."

"But you love Emma," Ellie gasped.

"I do, with all my heart, but if it's a choice between her or everyone else on the planet, then I'll do what's necessary."

"Well, I won't," Ellie declared hotly. "I'll find another way."

"What if there isn't one?"

"There's always another way."

"Is there?" Joanne asked. "I certainly hope so. It's not like I wanted any of this."

"So why did you let me grow up with her if you didn't want this? Surely it would have been easier to think about killing a stranger."

"That was Grammy's doing actually, or perhaps it was fate. Grandpa Harold's charge was Betty, Emma's nan, so Grammy enrolled me in the same school that Betty enrolled Sandra in. I don't suppose they ever expected us to hit it off or become so close."

"Grammy loved both Sandra and Emma. She wouldn't have ever harmed either of them."

"Yes, yes, she did. And she was like you. She always told Grandpa Harold he'd have to kill her before he could kill Emma. She always believed there was another way."

"And you never told Sandra any of this?"

"No, never. Bronwyn never told her child anything about her father. She grew up unaware of who she was related to, as did all of her descendants. Honestly, it didn't seem my place to tell Sandra anything."

"How've you kept it a secret from us all?"

"It wasn't hard; I just didn't talk about it. And none of the artefacts are here, so no one was ever going to stumble across them."

"Artefacts?"

"There's the prophecy and an angel blade. I suppose they're yours now. I'll have to take you to where they're hidden."

"Wait! How do you even know that Emma has the soul?"

"It's quite easy to work it out because it always skips a generation and because there's always a death in the family closely followed by a birth. Also, you can see it. Well, you and I can anyway because we're of the Guardian lineage."

"I've never seen Emma's soul."

"You have." Joanne nodded to emphasise her point. "You just didn't realise what you were seeing. Emma glows faintly, sometimes it's more pronounced than others, but it's always there. It's the soul. To be honest, it's too strong for the human body. From what I understand, most of Emma's line have died younger than normal because of it."

Ellie paled. "How much younger?"

It was Abaddon that answered, "Usually in their fifties, but it very much depends on how much they use the soul."

Ellie fell silent for a minute, trying to sort through everything she'd heard. She still had so many questions. "Mum," she said suddenly, "why our family? And why you? I mean, no offence, but in the movies this sort of thing is always passed to the oldest child. And how come you know Abaddon but I don't?"

"You'll have to ask Abaddon why she chose our family, and I honestly don't know why Grandpa Harold chose me instead of my brothers. I assume we all have angel blood running through our veins," Joanne answered, looking at Abaddon for confirmation.

"Could Uncle Clark and Uncle Dale see Emma for who she is then?"

"Maybe," Joanne said.

"No," Abaddon countered. "They have angel blood in their veins, but it has not been activated."

Joanne looked sharply at Abaddon. "I didn't know it had to be activated. How?"

"With an angel's kiss of course." Abaddon smirked as though the answer was obvious. "I've visited each of the chosen Guardians in turn, and to answer your other questions, Ellie, your family was chosen for geographical reasons only. They happened to live within striking distance of Bronwyn's cottage. And your mother knows me because her terror was too much to bear. When I arrived to give her the kiss, I found a terrified babe. It's the only time I've ever really intervened and provided comfort. Mind you, Joanne was the only one ever told as a child."

"When did you visit Ellie?" Joanne asked.

"The day she was born," Abaddon replied.

"Shouldn't you have waited until I'd told her? What if I'd had another child and chosen them to be the Guardian?"

Abaddon smiled gently at Joanne. "That was never going to happen. Eleanor's name is written into the prophecy. It has been in my mind since the beginning."

"Oh."

"So, erm, what's supposed to happen now?" Ellie asked.

"Now, you receive the angelic gifts and prepare for what you need to do. You must find a way to stop the portal from opening or else you'll spend your whole life fighting demons. The easiest solution is to nobble Emma," Abaddon answered.

"I still have no intention of doing that, but if you're so certain that's what needs to be done, why haven't you just done it already?"

Abaddon shrugged. "It's your destiny to find a solution, not mine. Now, for your gifts . . ." Abaddon stood, lifted her hand to her mouth, and blew in Ellie's direction. Even though Ellie hadn't seen her pick anything up, a fine dust tickled her nose making her sneeze.

"What did you just . . ." Ellie started to say before sneezing again. She glared at Abaddon angrily.

"What is it?" Joanne asked. "Abaddon, what did you do to Ellie?"

"I gave her the gift of sight," Abaddon answered without taking her eyes off Ellie. "Ellie, from this day forwards you'll always be able to see people for what they really are."

Ellie sneezed again before answering, "It's working, I think. I can see you. There are two of you, or rather I can see both of you. Man, this is complicated. One minute you're in your true form, the next you're just a girl having a drink."

"That will settle down in time, you'll learn to control the flicker. And now." She snapped her fingers.

Ellie flinched, expecting the blinding bright white light from earlier but instead pain shot through her body. It felt as though someone had hit her with a bolt of electricity; the current started where her heart was and flew outwards, up into her head, out into her arms, and down into her legs.

"Abaddon!" Joanne gasped.

"It's fine, chill. Her hair will settle down . . . eventually. She just needs to leave the conditioner on for a bit longer than normal tonight."

"What did you do?" Ellie forced the words out, the pain starting to fade.

"Nothing. Honestly you're just like your mother, always worrying. All I did was give you an edge. You're faster now, stronger. Your senses are heightened. And your hair really will be fine."

Ellie reached up and patted her head. An image of what she'd look like if she'd put her finger in a plug socket came to mind. Every single strand of hair appeared to be standing on end. She sighed and slumped forwards. "I guess I'm not going to Charlotte's cocktail party this weekend."

"Why would you say such a thing?" Abaddon exclaimed.

"With all this going on, I can't exactly go out and play, can I?"

"Why not? Life is for living. Tell her, Joanne, tell her."

"Well, maybe she should stay . . ."

"No! My blood flows in your veins. Do not make me regret giving it to your ancestors all those years ago. Besides, the prophecy says something about a new moon, so nothing's going to happen for at least a couple of weeks."

"Abaddon, I have another question," Ellie said, slowly lifting her head from the table. "Why are you doing all of this? Surely you want the portal open again so that you can go back home and be with your family?"

Abaddon stayed quiet for a moment before sighing quietly. "God spoke to me on the day that Blake was born. He gave me the prophecy and charged me with creating and caring for the Guardians. That's what I've done. Nothing more, nothing less."

"Maybe God isn't all that bad then?"

"Maybe not." Abaddon shrugged. "If he wanted to, though, he could do a whole lot more." Abaddon paused before adding, "But then again, so could I and so could you. Maybe God is just like us."

Chapter 9 – Emma

Sunday 14th April 2019

The third-floor apartment that Joanne had taken me and Ellie to was light and spacious, with huge picture windows overlooking the River Ribble. The journey over had been a little precarious because the wind monster that had claimed me as its own reared its ugly head a few times, but we'd survived. Joanne had looked increasingly alarmed until we were all safely inside the building, but to her credit, she didn't ask too many questions, not that I had any answers anyway.

The apartment was relatively small, with only one bedroom, an open-plan kitchen-living-dining space, and a bathroom, all of which had been decorated in shades of cream. Furniture had been kept to the bare minimum. In the bedroom, there were built-in wardrobes, which presumably had been in when Joanne had bought the place, a double bed, and a single bedside cabinet. The lounge was similarly made up with only a single three-seat sofa and an empty bookcase. It looked lived in but only just. There wasn't even a television or a radio. It looked like a show home, apart from the art supplies. Most of the available floor space was taken up with huge blank canvasses, and tubes of acrylic paint had been dumped around and about the place, even though Joanne had never shown any interest in art.

"Joanne, what's with all the bloody paint brushes?" I asked, although that wasn't what I really wanted to ask. Hundreds of questions had been circling in my mind ever since Ellie had rang me with the news. I felt like I was on the point of exploding. And not only did I have my own simmering rage to deal with, I could feel Blake's acting as an amplifier. How was it possible for Joanne, who was the epitome of a meek, mild-mannered, doting mother, to even think about ending my life? I mean I get it, I wasn't Ellie, I wasn't her actual daughter, but I'd always thought of her as a second mum. And all the while she'd been thinking about plunging a knife in my heart, or perhaps putting a bullet in my brain. I just couldn't wrap my head around it. She'd seemed so concerned about me when I'd been attacked, but now I realised that if only I'd have died, her problems would have been solved.

I hadn't wanted to come with Ellie this morning because of course Blake had relayed everything he'd heard and then I'd spoken to Ellie. We'd been on the phone for hours going over and over what she'd learned. While I was royally teed off, she felt hurt and betrayed. She was confused and in the end it was her need that had persuaded me to at least listen to what Joanne had to say, even though Blake had not been happy with my decision.

"I needed to tell the neighbours something. It's quite obvious I don't live here. In the end I told them I used the place as an art studio. They're quite used to me coming and going now." Joanne was sitting at the breakfast bar in the kitchen while I paced the length of the apartment and Ellie stared out of one of the many windows.

I stilled, hearing Joanne's words, absorbing their meaning and interpreting what she didn't say. She'd been serious about doing what needed to be done. The fight drained from me in an instant and I plopped down onto the sofa. It felt brand new. It'd probably never been used. "Why, Joanne? Why have you kept this to yourself all these years?"

"Because I had to, that's why," Joanne muttered, her head hung in defeat. Her whole life had been about keeping the most monumental of secrets, and she'd failed in her task. I looked over at her, her shoulders were slumped and there were dark bags under her eyes. Clearly she hadn't slept well either. A feeling of sorrow welled up inside me. Without thinking, I stood and quickly closed the gap between us. Before I could stop myself, I wrapped my arms around her. She held herself rigid for a brief moment before leaning into my hug.

Forever passed in a moment. No, I didn't understand how Joanne had kept everything from us, and obviously I didn't like the fact that she was so willing to 'do what was needed,' but her argument was a compelling one. She loved me (in fact she 'doted on me like a daughter' is what she'd said), but no one's life was more important than the fate of the world. Logically I couldn't disagree with her, I just didn't like the fact that it was my life on the line.

Eventually I pulled away. "Do you have tea making facilities here?" I asked.

Joanne wiped her eyes and nodded. "You'll find everything you need in the cupboard over the kettle, even powdered milk and cookies."

"Good." I squared my shoulders. "I don't know about anybody else, but I really need a brew and a biscuit right now."

"Count me in," Ellie said, joining me and her mum.

"And then, will you please tell me everything you know? I'd like to invite Blake here too. Is that okay?"

"Won't he be angry?"

"He's always angry," I answered, earning a snicker from Ellie.

Joanne looked at Ellie for reassurance before answering, "Sure. Why not?" she agreed, albeit reluctantly.

Blake, I called while filling the kettle at the sink. *Why don't you join us? Meet Joanne?*

She wants to kill you, he barked his reply.

I think she would say that she wants to save the world. There's a difference. Please, come and meet her. We need to understand what's going on so that we can come up with a plan of attack.

I could just end her life.

You could, but you won't. And even if you did, that wouldn't solve our problems. No matter what you do to Joanne, there's still the issue of you being used as a portal when the ritual is performed, whatever that means.

Blake didn't reply. He was not happy, but he did join us in the apartment. Of course, he chose to materialise with his scythe in hand. The butt of its pole rested gently on the floor, and the blade arced gracefully over his head. It glinted wickedly in the light of the room.

"Blake," I chastised. "That's really not necessary."

Ellie only stared, but Joanne gasped in fright. I tried to imagine what Blake looked like through her eyes; he was death incarnate after all.

"Blake," I hissed.

Again Blake didn't reply. He glared at me, shot a look at Joanne that would have thawed ice, and then casually placed the scythe back in the ether where it belonged.

"Erm, shouldn't we put that somewhere safe?" Joanne asked.

Blake continued to scowl at Joanne, leaving me to reply on his behalf. "It is safe, Joanne. You'll have to excuse him," I continued, placing a cup of tea in front of her. "He's a man of few words." The kettle had finished boiling while Blake had been showing off. "Do you want one?" I asked him, wiggling a cup in his direction.

"No," Blake answered. It seemed as though I was in the bad books too.

I finished making the tea and then sat back down on the sofa. Ellie joined me, leaving Blake standing and Joanne at the breakfast bar.

"Okay then, Joanne, it's over to you." I tried to make light of the situation, but ever since my bum had reconnected with the leather of the sofa, my emotions had ambushed me and my anxiety had ratcheted up a notch. Ellie must have sensed something was wrong because she reached over and gently patted my knee. Blake too must have known what I was feeling, but he didn't react or comment.

Joanne started speaking. She told the same tale that she'd told Ellie the day before. I knew because Ellie and I had already discussed it. It had all started with John and Bronwyn. Then came the split soul, Blake, and the original Key, at which point in time Abaddon had been told by God to create and care for a line of guardians. Over many centuries the Guardians had watched over the Key, knowing that if it was ever united with Blake then he could be used as a portal to the other dimensions, which would mean that angels and demons could overwhelm the earth.

"Have any of the Guardians ever seen Blake before now?" I asked when Joanne paused in her storytelling.

"Not as far as I know. We've only ever known who the Key was; you shine so brightly." Joanne smiled faintly at me.

"What about angels?"

"And demons?" Ellie chipped in.

"Again, not as far as I know. Apart from Abaddon, that is, but I think she's only ever spent time with me. Angels can take on any form; you could pass one in the street and never know. I assume demons can do the same."

"How do you get in touch with Abaddon?" I asked. I really wanted to meet her. Ellie had painted quite the colourful picture of her.

"You don't get in touch with Abaddon. She gets in touch with you when she wants to."

"Huh," I muttered, "bummer."

"Mum," Ellie interjected, "when did you buy this place?" Clearly she still had questions of her own.

"How do you know I didn't inherit it from Grandpa Harold?"

"Come on, Mum, if Grandpa Harold had ever owned this place, it wouldn't be quite so sterile."

"It's not sterile," Joanne protested, "it's functional."

Ellie didn't answer but her raised eyebrows spoke volumes.

"Fine, it's sterile. But I only come here once or twice a week to check on things. I usually sit and read my book for a couple of hours to keep up the pretence of being a jobbing artist."

"So, when did you buy it?"

"After Grandpa Harold died. He left me some money and of course, the artefacts."

"Why didn't you just keep the prophecy and the angel blade at home?"

"I didn't want them there. I didn't want them polluting the air we breathe, just like I didn't want you to be a part of all this. I half hoped it wasn't even true. I mean I knew it was, because of Abaddon, you see, but I've prayed over and over again that Emma was just little old Emma, that you didn't have angel blood in your veins, that I'd never have to bring you here. All I've ever wanted is to live a normal life, to grow old with your dad and watch you get married and have children of your own."

"Can we see them?" I interrupted.

"See what?" I guess I hadn't exactly been explicit.

"The prophecy and the angel blade."

"Oh, sure . . . I guess."

"What's the problem?"

"It's just . . . I'm not sure . . . I mean, I thought they were for Ellie's eyes only."

"It's okay," Ellie cut in. "I think we're past all that now. Emma can see them too."

"And what about . . ." Joanne flicked her eyes in the direction of Blake, who'd stood unmoving throughout the whole of her monologue, his emotions in disarray. From our conversations, I knew that there was so much he hadn't even been aware of: the three dimensions, angels, demons, the fact that he was—or at the very least could be used as—a portal into Heaven and Hell. Confusion waged war on anger, and so he'd held his tongue.

"Blake too," Ellie confirmed.

Still looking unsure, Joanne dutifully stood and retrieved the artefacts. She didn't have to go far; they'd been stashed in a kitchen drawer all along.

"Mum," Ellie gasped, rising to her feet to investigate, "shouldn't you have put them in a safe?"

"It's okay, no one knows about them. No one knows about any of this."

"That's not quite true, though, is it?" Ellie argued. "Abaddon told us that there are people who know who Emma is and that they want to use her to get to Blake. It stands to reason that they also know who we are."

Joanne only shrugged before laying a curious-looking scroll and a relatively plain dagger on the kitchen counter. Ellie reached for the scroll and Blake stepped forward to pick up the dagger. It was sheathed in a black cover that fitted perfectly over the blade, butting right up against the hilt. The handle was a polished wood, exactly like the pole of Blake's scythe. Blake wasted no time in removing the cover and lifting it to his eyes for a closer inspection.

Joanne gasped aloud. "I've never seen it before."

"Never?" Ellie and I asked at exactly the same time.

"No. I keep telling you, I never wanted any part of any of this. I did as I was told. I kept the secret, I kept those . . . those things safe, but I've never looked at them. I only know as much as I do because of Abaddon."

The blade was absolutely stunning. It was only six or eight inches in length, but while it could be said to be lacking on the length front, it made up for that with its looks. It was pearlescent in colour and easily caught the light from the windows. Milky white, baby pink, and minty green swirled together, changing the blade's look with every movement that Blake made.

"It looks just like Abaddon's wings," Ellie remarked.

"So, what does the prophecy say?" I asked, tearing my eyes away from the angel blade, assuming it was about me.

"It's gibberish," Ellie answered, having mastered the art of dealing with a scroll that had been tightly bound for many years.

"It's written in an angelic script," Joanne interjected. "It says: *Behold! That which was torn asunder will be reunited in the light of a new moon. And in the days that follow, the beast will be set free.* At least that's what Abaddon told me it said."

"There could be more to it then?"

"In point of fact, I would assume there is," Joanne replied. "Abaddon never told me that Ellie's name was written into the prophecy until yesterday, so there's that at least."

"The scroll is certainly long enough to say more," Ellie agreed with her mum.

"What else has Abaddon told you over the years?" It was my turn to ask a question.

"Nothing really. I think you know everything I know now," Joanne answered. "There is one more thing that I want you to know, though, Emma." She joined me on the sofa and took my hand in hers. "I do love you, you know? I always have done, and I always will do."

"But you were willing to kill me?" I couldn't help myself from asking the question.

Joanne shifted uncomfortably in her seat before nodding her head ever so slightly. I might have missed it if I hadn't been looking directly at her. "If it makes you feel any better, though, I've prayed and prayed that you wouldn't ever meet Blake. If only you hadn't," she finished sadly.

There was something in her voice that made me look her squarely in the eyes, but before I could say or do anything further, Blake was across the room and had lifted me from where I'd been sat. He pushed me behind him, shielding my body with his own. Next to him, I felt small. "What . . . what's going on?" I asked. The atmosphere in the room had changed so suddenly, becoming charged. Electricity crackled in the air.

"I tried to tell you that she was going to kill you," Blake replied, passing the angel blade to me and pulling his scythe from the ether, gripping it firmly with both hands.

"Mum!" Ellie gasped, rushing over from the kitchen unit. "Please tell me you didn't?" She pulled something from her mum's hand. It was only then that I saw the syringe. It was full of a clear liquid. "What's in this?"

"It's nothing; it's not what you think." Joanne half stood, reaching for Ellie before slumping back onto the sofa, wringing her hands together in anguish. Tears flowed freely down her face.

"What. Is. It?" Ellie demanded.

"It's just a sleeping potion. I was only ever going to knock her out."

I gasped in shock while Blake responded, "Liar," he spat.

"Is it, Mum? Is it just a sleeping potion?" Ellie asked, holding the syringe up to her own neck.

"No, no, please don't. Ellie, I beg you. Don't press the plunger."

"What's in the syringe, Mum?" Ellie asked again. Her voice was remarkably calm.

"It's a poison. Emma wouldn't have felt anything; she'd have just fallen asleep and then her heart would have stopped beating. It was going to be peaceful."

"Peaceful?" I exploded. "You really were going to kill me!"

"Emma, don't you see? It's you or the world. I never wanted this. I never dreamed I'd actually have to go through with what I'd promised, but I was told that if you ever met Blake, it was game over. As soon as they get their hands on you—and they will—they'll force you to do the ritual. The portal will be opened and the devil himself will walk the earth. You don't want that, do you?"

"Well, no . . ." I answered honestly, my rage dying away, confusion taking its place. "But I also don't want to die." Hot, wet tears of frustration were trailing down my own face now.

"Mum, I think you should go," Ellie stated. Her words sounded cold.

"Ellie, please. Think about this. Think about the options."

"I will find a way to save Emma and the world. I will not harm a hair on her head. She's my best friend. Now please, will you just go before Blake decides he's had enough?"

It was Joanne's turn to gasp. In the midst of pleading with Ellie, she seemed to have forgotten about the menace that hovered beside her, desperate to prove that he could in fact take swift and decisive action when required, when my life was threatened.

Blake, please don't hurt her, I begged silently.

After what she's done?

Yes, even after what she's done. She's Ellie's mum. You can't hurt her; it will kill Ellie.

"Mum, please go," Ellie said again, pulling Joanne to her feet and ushering her to the front door.

"Will you be coming home tonight?"

"I don't know. I might stay with Emma for a couple of nights."

"Ellie, please come home. We need to talk."

"No," Ellie stated plainly. "Right now you need to go home. And I'll come home when I'm good and ready." She firmly propelled Joanne across the threshold and then slammed the door behind her before collapsing on the floor in tears.

Chapter 10 – Blake

Sunday 14ᵗʰ April 2019

Blake stood in the exact centre of the Piazza San Marco, Venice. A sea of tourists milled around him, pushing each other aside in their insatiable desire to see and photograph each of the landmarks of the city. Blake was facing his favourite, the Basilica di San Marco, the imposing Italo-Byzantine church that dominated the city. It had stood, in one guise or another, for longer than he'd been alive, and Blake liked things that were older than he was. The queue to enter, and eyeball the treasures within, snaked its way backwards and forwards in a tightly compressed zig-zag in front of the building before trailing off towards the Doge's Palace, the pink and white façade of which gleamed brightly in the weak springtime sun.

Street sellers hawked their wares, ignoring the locals but pressing day-trippers and weekenders to buy both Venetian masks and pigeon food, which only served to draw the birds in among the crowd, where they threatened to trip up anyone and everyone, apart from Blake, of course.

Blake hadn't needed Emma to ask him to give her and Ellie some space. As Emma had rushed to Ellie's side, Blake had simply stepped out of the room. He'd ended up in Venice because he'd needed to be somewhere busy, somewhere where he could lose himself in the crowd.

Blake was livid with Joanne, but he was also furious at Emma. He'd told her what Joanne had planned as soon as it had become a possibility, in the early hours of the morning when the idea had first occurred to her. Emma's death hadn't been guaranteed, in fact the likelihood of Joanne going through with her scheme had been quite remote. The probability had been less than five percent, almost as though Joanne herself was unsure whether or not to act, but it had been there all the same. And Emma had refused to listen. She'd been unable to accept that Joanne would ever harm her, choosing instead to believe that Blake must be mistaken. Him? Mistaken? He'd never been mistaken about anything in the whole of his very long, very depressing life.

Blake clenched his fists tightly together and bellowed his frustration aloud. Nobody flinched. In fact, a group of girls nearby burst out laughing before crowding together to take a selfie against the backdrop of the Venetian skyline.

"Seith," Blake spoke quietly, needing the companionship that only Seith could offer before he went insane with rage.

Unusually Seith didn't simply materialise. Instead the beast came trotting around the corner of the Campanile. Standing at 323 feet, it was the tallest structure within Venice, the 'El Paron de Casa.' It succeeded in making even Seith look small. The dog's head hung low as it weaved its way through the crowd towards Blake, its movements fluid, its steps deliberate. People moved to one side without knowing why, with only the sense of a shadow blocking the sun for a brief moment. Eventually Seith reached Blake and sat in front of him.

"Demons, Seith. There are demons." There was no point in Blake venting at Seith, he knew full well that, despite looking savage, Seith would advise calm and acquiescence.

While he listened to Seith's reply, Blake focussed his thoughts on Emma, the way the sun set her hair ablaze, the sparkle in her eyes when she was happy, the feel of her lips on his . . . . In no time at all the living disappeared, replaced by a swarm of silvery-coloured souls. One or two were marred with darkness, but in the main they were beacons of pure light.

"You won't find any," a voice declared beside him.

Blake glanced around, his vision returning to normal. Standing beside Seith was a petite woman, with long dark hair twisted into a bun at the back of her head. She had her hands on her hips and most definitely appeared to be talking to him. There was only one possible explanation.

"Abaddon, I assume."

"In the flesh." Abaddon smiled brightly. Dark makeup outlined her eyes and she wore a brick red colour on her lips. "Well, that's not exactly true, of course. My own flesh looks a little different, but I like this outfit. It's petite and lithe, the boys can't resist. Actually neither can the girls." She giggled brightly before pausing, waiting for some kind of response from Blake, but he held his tongue. "Oh, come now, Blake, don't be like that," she continued. "It's not my fault that you didn't know we exist. If you want to blame anyone, blame your father."

"My father?"

"Yes, he was our jailor after all. The gatekeeper of the dimensions."

"Who?"

"John. Your father. Wakey wakey! Surely you've worked out by now that John was your father, just like Bronwyn was Emma's ultimate grandmother. It makes you think, doesn't it?" She arched her eyebrows before winking at Blake, but he chose to ignore her. "Oh, Blaaakeeey!" Abaddon whined, clenching her fists and stamping her foot on the ground. In an instant the Piazza San Marco fell silent, everybody stilled, frozen in time. Blake whirled in a circle, his coattails lifting in the breeze. Even the pigeons had fallen silent. "Neat little trick, isn't it?" Abaddon laughed aloud.

"What did you do?" Blake asked.

"It's nothing for you to worry about. I just wanted some time alone with you."

"No one can see us anyway."

"That's not quite true, they can't see you or Seith, but they can see me."

"How . . .?"

"Oh don't you worry your pretty little head about that. We've more important things to talk about. You see, the thing is, I'm rather fond of the guardian line. If anything were to happen to it, I'd be most displeased."

"I would never hurt Ellie."

"And Joanne?"

Blake couldn't bring himself to reply, but the corner of his lip lifted in distaste and a sneer marred his face.

"Blakey, darling, if anything happens to Joanne, you will suffer more than you've ever suffered before."

"You can't hurt me."

"You'd be surprised at what I can and cannot do. Now, consider yourself warned," she finished before snapping her fingers. Life returned to normal in the Venetian capital, and without another word, Abaddon skipped off into the crowd, leaving Blake and Seith to ponder her words.

Chapter 11 – Emma

Friday 19th April 2019 (Good Friday)

The day of Charlotte's cocktail party turned out to be a beautiful one weather-wise. Of course I couldn't really enjoy it all that much because every time I set foot outside of my house, I was ambushed by what felt like hurricane-level winds.

"This is ridiculous," I complained to Blake. "Have you ever come across anything like this before?"

"No," he answered, his voice flat. He was still brooding about everything that had happened in the last few days. Mind you, I hadn't exactly come to terms with it all either. Ghosts were real, angels and demons walked the earth, and Joanne had tried to kill me! I couldn't get over that last one. And poor Ellie was in bits. Since last Sunday, we'd been over and over what had happened but neither one of us could wrap our heads around it. Ellie at least had work to occupy herself, but I had nothing to distract myself with. Foolishly, I'd voiced that complaint to Ellie, and as a consequence, we were still going to Charlotte's shindig despite living in the wonderfully-weird-world-of-Angelic-Visitors-and-Murderous-Mums.

I'd tried to persuade Ellie that going to Charlotte's was a bad idea, but she'd become increasingly adamant. In her words, she wanted to 'go out, get drunk, and forget about the last week.' And ultimately, while I didn't plan on getting drunk myself, I couldn't blame her for wanting to wallow in the anaesthetic qualities of alcohol for at least one evening.

"What are you doing?" I asked Blake, glancing over my shoulder before turning my attention back to the little pest I'd been watching through the kitchen window. The 'little pest' was Cooper; he was happily making himself a nest in one of my borders, trampling down some of my most beautiful plants to make his chosen spot in the sunshine more comfortable. When he was satisfied, he curled himself into a ball, yawned, and closed his eyes. Blake, on the other hand, had his nose in the fridge.

"Looking." Blake was not the most articulate of people at the best of times.

"Looking at what?" I turned to face him.

"Where are the strawberries?"

"You ate them yesterday," I replied.

He huffed his reply.

"Why don't you help me make my cocktail for tonight?"

"Why can't I come?"

"I've told you already, it's a girl's night."

"I could change my appearance, become female for the night."

"Please don't." I shuddered at the thought.

"I don't like leaving you."

"I'll be fine; I'll be with Ellie."

Blake sighed. "I've never been to a party."

"You've been to plenty of parties."

"I've never been to one where people could see me."

"Hmmm, well, there isn't anything I can do about that, I'm afraid. Now, are you helping me or not?"

Charlotte hadn't asked us to take anything for the party, but I'd stumbled across a fruity-looking recipe that I wanted to try. It was for a mocktail rather than a cocktail, but that suited me just fine. I was more of a tea girl anyway, although I could always squeeze in a milk chocolate Frappuccino with an extra shot of chocolate, or an indulgent hot chocolate topped off with whipped cream and marshmallows.

"What are you making?" Blake asked, emphasising the word 'you.' He clearly had no intention of playing chef's assistant.

"A Forager's Fizz," I answered, searching for the recipe on my phone.

As predicted, Blake didn't help. He did sample, though, regularly and by unashamedly dipping his finger into the mixture—hygiene rules be damned!

First of all, I had to make a rosehip and juniper berry syrup. Blake declared the rosehips to be like cranberries, the juniper to be like a citrus-infused pine cone (although when he'd ever had a citrus-infused pine cone was beyond me), and the resultant gloopy liquid to be nice and sweet. After that I had to make a blackberry shrub.

"Curses," I swore, reading the method on my phone. It was meant to be left to macerate for forty-eight hours, and I didn't have forty-eight hours spare.

"It won't make any difference to the taste," Blake declared, suddenly an expert.

"Do you actually know that because you've reaped someone who made this in their lifetime, or are you just guessing?" I asked.

"Both."

"It can't be both, which is it?"

"I've seen people making this before. Some left the shrub to macerate, some didn't. None of them complained, so I am *guessing* it doesn't matter. I'd like to say I'd tasted it before but well . . ." He shrugged his shoulders rather than finishing.

"Oh sod it then." The blackberries I used were ones that I'd harvested (and subsequently frozen) from my own garden last season. I mixed them with the required amount of sugar, nuked them in the microwave to dissolve as much of the sugar as possible, and then strained them to separate the pulp from the liquid. The pulp was binned, and then I whisked the liquid with an equal amount of red wine vinegar. Blake appropriated the vinegar bottle after I'd finished with it and sniffed its contents.

"I really wouldn't drink that if I were you," I cautioned, but Blake ignored me lifting the bottle to his lips and tipping it back. He quickly gagged while I laughed out loud. "What? I did try to warn you," I said, trying to compose myself when Blake's displeasure speared me like a knife.

"Finish your cocktail," was all the response I got.

"All that's left is to combine the ingredients with some sparkling water. I'll do that at the party. I'm tempted to use lemonade, though, I think that will taste nicer," I finished, turning to look at Blake. A ripple of lust washed over me. Blake was without a doubt the most gorgeous man I'd ever laid eyes on, even when he was brooding. He was tall and broad with dark hair that fell to his shoulders and smouldering eyes. He was dressed in his preferred attire: black knee-high boots, black trousers, black shirt, and a black jacket that was covered in delicate embroidery.

Blake's emotions mirrored my own, and as we bounced our desire between us, a pressure started to build within me. The intensity grew until I was on the verge of exploding. Only then did Blake close the gap. Leaving mere millimetres between us, he laid the briefest of kisses on my lips.

"Aren't you bothered about what Abaddon said?" I asked.

"No."

"She did intimate that we're effectively siblings."

"There are many generations between us. We're nothing like brother and sister," Blake concluded before kissing me again.

"Mmm," I hummed, sighing in satisfaction and stepping in to press my body against his. A nagging doubt still writhed away at the back of my mind, but nothing about my relationship with Blake was normal. He was almost a thousand years old, and I was not yet thirty. Did it matter if our families had been connected centuries before?

For most of the afternoon I explored Blake's body, kissing and caressing every inch of his skin, losing myself in our lovemaking, wondering if he really could change his entire look in much the same way that he could change his attire. Blake was an incorporeal being, forced to manifest when he was close to me. Outside of my bubble, his essence could be shaped however he desired. He looked like he did simply because that was how he believed himself to look.

"Blake?" I asked, breaking into the sleepy silence that had fallen. At some point we'd made it up to my bedroom and lay nestled in each other's arms wrapped in the quilt. Well, I was wrapped in the quilt, snug as a bug in a rug. Blake was not. When I'd said I was cold, he'd said he was hot; so when I'd wrapped the quilt around me, he'd pulled only a sliver of it over himself, which suited me just fine. "Tell me about ghosts." I didn't want to dwell on anything else.

"They're called remnants," he replied.

"You said that before. Does it really matter what we call them?"

"Yes. Ghosts are a Hollywood invention; they don't exist. They are spectral recreations of the living, unable to move on because of some misbegotten tie to those left living. They are almost always portrayed as being malicious, or in most cases evil. Remnants are a little bit like me, although they don't have souls."

"Huh, I always assumed ghosts—"

"Remnants," Blake corrected.

"Whatever," I muttered. "I always thought *remnants* were souls that hadn't been collected." As soon as the words left my mouth, I knew I'd made a mistake. Blake's anger spiked, stabbing me in the heart. He stiffened and started to pull away from the little nest we'd made, but I clung onto him, working to pacify him before he could even start to protest. "I didn't mean that exactly as it sounded. Of course I know now that that can't possibly be the case, I'm just saying that that's what I'd always assumed before meeting you," I paused, concentrating on how Blake was feeling for a moment. "Come on," I wheedled. "Teach me," I offered, trusting in Blake's love of all things specific. "If they aren't souls, what are they?"

Blake's temper abated, although I didn't need our emotional connection to know that he hadn't totally forgiven me. His body remained tense next to mine, however he did explain what a remnant was. "As you know, when a person dies, I collect their soul . . ." Of course he had to start there! ". . . but their spirit can remain behind. Sometimes spirits linger here for days, sometimes they linger for years."

"What's a spirit, and how's it different from a soul?"

"A spirit is the essence of an individual. It's each person's identity, their own unique sense of self. As people grow and mature, their spirit becomes infused with some of the energy of creation from their soul. It becomes an entity in its own right. In most cases, it simply withers and dies along with the body after death, but sometimes it doesn't, sometimes it becomes a remnant, capable of existing without a body. It's everything the person was but without a body or a soul."

"So everyone has a body, a spirit, and a soul?" I asked. This was complicated stuff we were talking about.

"Correct."

"And when the body dies, you collect the soul but the spirit chooses for itself whether to live on or die?"

"It's not a conscious choice."

"Go on," I prompted.

"For most people, death is a welcome release, the body is tired or in pain and the person is ready to move on. As a consequence, the spirit dies with the body. Remnants occur when the body and the spirit are out of sync."

"Do all remnants come from younger people then?"

"A bigger percentage of them, yes. But sometimes older people are not finished living their lives. They can become remnants too."

"Are they dangerous?"

"No. Why would you ask that?"

"If I was being haunted, that would explain the wind monster attacks, wouldn't it?"

"No. They don't attack people; they just live their lives. Anyway as I said before, they tend to avoid me. I'm sure they'll avoid you too."

"Hmmm," I replied, falling silent to think through what Blake had explained. "Why . . ." I opened my mouth to ask another question but was rudely interrupted by an alarm sounding. "What time is it?" I asked, even though it was as easy for me to look at the time as it was for Blake to do so, never mind the fact that I'd set the alarm, so I actually knew what time it was if I thought about it.

"Five o' clock."

"Urgh. I'd best get up and get ready for this party then," I replied, sitting up and switching off the alarm, which was annoyingly persistent. I couldn't quite bring myself to head straight for a shower though. Left to my own devices, I wouldn't even be going to this party; too much had happened in the last ten days. Never mind the fact Charlotte was hosting it.

In the bathroom, while the shower heated up, I stood butt naked looking into the mirror, wanting to see any one of the women who had had my soul before me. The past week had been a little on the strange side, but other than my nan's warning, the ladies had been noticeable by their absence. I closed my eyes, scrunched up my face, and held the pose for what felt like hours but was actually only seconds before checking my reflection. Success! Although the face that stared back at me was not one that I'd seen before. If I had to guess, I would have said the lady in question was from the turn of the century. Perhaps my great nan. She was quite plainly dressed in a high neck shirt that had ballooned sleeves and a frilly 'bib.' She wore very little makeup, but her hair was elegantly rolled, twisted, and pinned so that it was completely off her face. She looked prim, proper, and demure.

Beware, Emma. Darkness surrounds you, she whispered.

"My nan said that," I answered, not really expecting a response; the ladies tended to prefer one-liners. "I wish I knew what she was referring to though. Quite a lot has happened recently." I, on the other hand, preferred two-way conversations.

Only your home is safe, she continued.

"Good to know. Why's that then?"

It has been cleansed in preparation for what they want to do to you. But it means you're safe from the darkness at least. She started to fade as condensation formed on the mirror.

"Wait! Who's 'they'? And are 'they' not the darkness?" I asked, the pitch of my voice rising into a shriek.

For now, the darkness must be your primary concern, she replied before disappearing completely just as the door was yanked open from outside. A cold draft tickled at my skin, causing goose bumps to erupt.

"What's wrong?" Blake demanded to know.

"You can literally hear my thoughts. Don't you know already?" I huffed sarcastically, even though it was fear that snaked its way through my gut and not annoyance.

Blake just shrugged. "I'll remain while you shower," he stated.

"Fine," I answered, feeling confused. When I was being stalked, I hadn't ever been bothered about being on my own. To be honest, it hadn't even occurred to me that I might be safer with others. Something about my great nan's warning had me on edge though. Maybe the difference was that I'd never fully committed to the idea that anything untoward was happening when I was being stalked, not until it was too late anyway. I'd driven myself completely and utterly crazy with the conflicting thoughts. There was no mistaking the warning in my great nan's words though. I was in danger. Again. And it seemed as though there were multiple sources of danger this time. Joy. Before I could worry about that, I had to get through Charlotte's party.

I hurried in the shower because I'd dawdled for so long before getting in it, although by 'hurried,' I still took the time to shampoo my hair before applying a conditioning treatment that needed to be left in for three minutes. And seeing as I was going out, I shaved, scrubbed my skin with an exfoliating shower gel, cleaned my nails, and did a mini facial.

"Blake, what time is it?" I asked, turning the tap off before the water could run cold.

"I am not your personal timekeeping device," he answered, "but it's nearly six."

"Crap, really?" I asked, ignoring his jibe. If I picked him up on every single one of his I-am-not-your-personal-insert-whatever-here comments, we'd never not be arguing. Ellie was picking me up at 6:45 p.m., I needed to get a move on.

To expedite the process, I rough blow-dried my hair, knotted it at the back of my head in a loose bun, and secured it with pins. I kept my makeup to a minimum, taking inspiration from my great nan, and then pulled on my version of a little black dress, a 1950s inspired knee-length fit and flare with a deep 'V' at its neck and little cap sleeves. Ellie had been adamant about the dressing up thing. I was just doing battle with a pair of sheer tights when a car horn sounded. I quickly yanked them up, wincing at the ripping sound that followed, and shoved my feet into a pair of low-heeled shoes.

"Well?" I said to Blake, who'd sat quietly watching as I'd gotten myself ready.

"Very nice," he replied. "I still don't think this is a good idea."

"Me either, but Ellie wants to go. And I'll be fine. I'll be with Ellie the whole time. Besides, you can't sense death in my future," I stated, making an assumption. "Can you?" I asked to confirm.

"No, but—"

"There you go then," I interrupted, giving him a quick kiss. When I thought back to his words later on, I heartily wished I'd paid attention to his little 'but,' but in the heat of the moment, I rushed down the stairs and out of the door, pausing only to give the boys some sweeties each and to grab what I needed to take with me: the Forager's Fizz I'd made earlier on in the day, some lemonade to mix with it, my phone, and a jacket.

Chapter 12 – Emma

Friday 19ᵗʰ April 2019 (Good Friday)

Charlotte's cocktail party was less 'party' and more 'social gathering' in my humble opinion. But that was okay. In fact, that worked better for me. The only guests (besides me and Ellie) were Rhona, Angela, and Tori. The five of us were gathered together while our hostess busied herself in the kitchen, readying the food. With the exception of Charlotte, we'd all known each other for quite some time, and despite the fact that I hadn't wanted to come, I found myself relaxing and having fun.

The journey over had been a little on the hairy side, mind you. My pet wind monster had hurled itself against the car a couple of times, but Ellie—nervous driver that she was—had somehow managed to hold the wheel steady, and we'd made it in one piece.

Charlotte's house had a homely, comfortable quality to it, albeit it was a little on the cluttered side for me. Every single nook and cranny was filled with something or other. In the living room, one whole wall was lined with shelving that was literally stuffed full with books. Opposite was a fireplace that was adorned with candles. And underneath the bay window there was a two-tiered coffee table that was piled high with magazines. In the corner between the fireplace and the coffee table, a small flatscreen television had been squeezed in, and next to that a pile of DVDs was growing up the wall, much like how ivy would grow up the side of a house.

The seating options were mismatched and strewn about in a seemingly haphazard fashion. In front of the shelves there was a dark red three-seat sofa that had clearly seen better days but wasn't quite threadbare. In the far corner there was an easy chair that was almost (but not quite) the same colour as the sofa, and in front of the television there were a couple of straight-backed dining chairs. The curtains had been drawn before me and Ellie had arrived, and as a consequence, the lounge could have been quite gloomy. Instead, it was made cosy by the addition of a string of fairy lights entwined along and around the shelving.

All in all—and if I'm honest, I absolutely, most definitely did not want to admit this—I'd found myself warming to Charlotte. She'd proven herself to be a welcoming and generous hostess. Either that or she had a drinking problem because there were bottles and bottles of gin, vodka, rum, Prosecco, and both red and white wine to go at! Her dining room table had been groaning with food before she'd gone off to heat up the hot food, and she was making cocktails to order. She was, without a doubt, better at entertaining than I was. I tended to make people their first drink and then left them to get on with it. Or else I didn't invite anyone over in the first place on the premise that Cooper and Watson didn't like strangers.

Upon arriving, I'd handed my Forager's Fizz over and then graciously accepted a glass of it back, although instead of lemonade, Ellie had insisted it be mixed with Prosecco. She'd accepted a Strawberry Daiquiri and then we'd joined our friends. The conversation had flowed easily enough without any awkward moments.

"Have you all seen the new live action *Dumbo* yet?" Rhona asked.

"No, I haven't," Angela and Tori replied pretty much together.

"The trailers look so cute," Angela went on to say.

"Well, what could possibly be cuter than a baby elephant with ears bigger than his own body?" Tori agreed.

"Erm, let me think about that for a minute . . ." Ellie faked a thinking face. "How about Daniel Craig in *Casino Royale*?"

"Ellie!" I exclaimed, although I couldn't help but laugh along with everyone else. "Honestly you dive straight into the gutter every time."

"You fancy him too," she deadpanned. I knew from the drive over that Ellie was far from okay, but she was putting on a good show.

"I don't, not anymore at least," I declared, piously thinking of Blake.

"Isn't he on your list?" Angela broke into mine and Ellie's back and forth.

"I don't have a list now. I don't need one," I answered.

"Ooh, this new boyfriend of yours must be super hot then. When do we get to meet him?" Tori asked.

"Soon," I promised. "He's just a bit, erm . . . shy," I answered. My relationship with Blake hadn't been kept a secret, but I'd never really thought about him meeting that many people. I certainly had no intention of explaining who he was, so how exactly would that go? What do you do for a living, Blake? Reap the souls of the dying. Interesting.

And does that pay well? Not exactly, but seeing as I don't need to eat or drink, it's enough. "I might just go and see how Charlotte's getting on," I excused myself, hoisting myself out of the seat I'd bagsied on arrival.

Charlotte's house wasn't overly large. I found my way to the kitchen with relative ease, giving myself a silent round of applause for escaping one awkward situation only to land myself in another. Being the master of greetings, I announced my presence with a simple 'hey.'

"Oh hi, do you want another drink?" Charlotte glanced my way briefly before turning back to what she was doing. She looked a little harried. She was obviously sweating and tendrils of hair had escaped from what had been a particularly neat French braid not that long ago.

"I can wait," I replied. "Are you okay? You look stressed."

"No, no, I'm fine. As long as everyone's okay and doesn't need any more drinks, I'm fine."

"Erm, okay, but maybe I can help?"

"You're my guest; I couldn't possibly ask you to help." A pained look danced fleetingly across her face, only to be replaced by what was obviously a forced grin.

"I don't mind. You'd be saving me from Angela and Tori; they want to know all about Blake."

"Ah yes, the mysterious boyfriend. He's been quite the topic of conversation over the last few weeks. The girls are dying to meet him."

"Hmmm." I drifted further into the kitchen to see what it was that Charlotte was struggling with.

"Don't you want to show him off?"

"Blake is . . ." I faltered, not really knowing how to explain it.

"It's okay, you don't have to explain anything to me. You're entitled to your privacy."

"It's not that I don't want people to meet Blake, it's just . . . he can be . . ." Without saying the words 'he's the Grim Reaper and can only exist in my bubble,' I had literally no idea how to explain away the fact that I didn't want Blake to meet many of my friends. As I struggled to find the words, it suddenly dawned on me that I didn't want the hassle of introducing him to anyone else. I'd just about accepted that my heart and soul literally belonged to the man, but there was no denying the fact that he could be a smidge challenging when he wanted to be. Although he'd lived a very long life (a point of fact that I tried not to dwell on), in many ways he was like a newborn (not in the ways that mattered, mind you). Quite frankly his behaviour was unlikely to ever be socially acceptable, a fact that I'd accepted but would everyone else? I'd had to school him carefully on what was and was not allowed to do before we'd gone to Grammy's funeral.

"Do you love him?" Charlotte asked, turning to face me fully, laying aside her task.

"I think so." I was starting to believe that I did, but I figured Blake deserved to hear it first.

"Then does it matter what anyone else thinks of him?"

"I . . . I never said it did."

"You didn't, but you were thinking it, weren't you?"

"My thoughts might have meandered along that route," I admitted, fidgeting where I stood.

Charlotte laughed wryly. "It was written all over your face. I've worn that look before; I recognised it easily enough." She rolled her eyes, perhaps realising that she was advising me to do something she'd evidently failed at.

"Have you? Why?" I didn't even think about the fact that I was essentially prying.

"I'm gay."

"Oh. Why would that be an issue?" Maybe Blake wasn't the only one who needed a lesson in conversational dos and don'ts. I really had to teach my mouth some manners sometime soon or else learn to engage my brain before I spoke. Charlotte's personal affairs were none of my business. I hadn't ever shown her the slightest bit of warmth before tonight; nothing gave me the right to ask such intimate questions. "I'm sorry, Charlotte, it's—"

"It's okay," she interrupted. "I want you to know. I always got the impression that you were wary of me, and I want us to be friends. I like Cedar's, I'd like to stay, and that means we'll be working together for a long time."

I winced but didn't actually answer.

"You were wary of me." Charlotte arched an eyebrow at me.

"I'm sorry, I really am. I just . . . I always got the impression you were hiding something. I even thought that perhaps you were the one who was stalking me." I seized the opportunity that had been presented to me to get the truth out into the open.

The blood drained from Charlotte's face. "Why would you think that? I'd never . . . I wouldn't . . . it was just a crush." Her hands flew up to cover her mouth as she realised exactly what she'd admitted.

"You have a crush on me?" I asked, beyond stunned.

"Had. I had a crush on you."

"Charlotte, that's . . . nice." What else did you say in this situation?

"I'm over it. I've actually started seeing someone new recently."

"Good, good."

"Why did you think I was stalking you?"

"Mostly because of your car."

"But Matthew drives the same make and model as I do."

"Yes, I know, but your family owns a florists, and I did receive that bouquet of roses."

"Tenuous."

"I know that now." I paused, unsure what else to say. I'd just admitted to wrongfully accusing Charlotte of stalking me and subsequently found out she'd had a thing for me. If there had ever been a class on how to handle such situations, I'd missed it. "Do you want me to go?" I asked eventually.

"No, please don't. I'm glad you were honest with me. Maybe we can start afresh now. Friends?" She graciously held out her hand, but I ignored her peace offering, choosing instead to give her a quick hug.

"I really am sorry," I apologised, genuinely meaning it. "Now, what's got you so frazzled in the kitchen?"

Charlotte nibbled at her lip before answering. "I think I bit off more than I can chew. I've got a bunch of stuff to heat up, and I still need to ice the cake. I ran out of time this afternoon."

"Let me ice the cake for you. That way you can focus on what needs to go in the oven and at what time."

"Do you really not mind?"

"Absolutely not! It won't look fantastic, but if you have some Nutella in, it will taste amazing."

"That cupboard over there." Charlotte indicated one of the lower ones. "Knock yourself out."

Charlotte and I spent a happy few minutes in the kitchen working alongside each other and chatting about everything and nothing. I was surprised to learn that she tended to keep her sexuality quiet because she'd experienced prejudice and bullying in the past.

"But it's 2019," I exclaimed, horrified that some people still had homophobic views.

"And?"

"I thought people were more accepting nowadays."

"Some of them are, but I've been called names and once I had faecal matter pushed through my letterbox. It's made me cautious about who I tell."

"That's disgusting. Who would do such a thing?"

"Who indeed. Society is not nearly as advanced as most people would like to believe."

"Yeah, I get that. I—"

"What are you two doing in here?" Ellie asked from the door. "Tori says she's getting hungry."

"I think we're just about there, aren't we, Charlotte?" I looked at the cake I'd iced and wondered how I'd managed to make such a mess. The cake was liberally covered in frosting and sprinkles, but so too was the worktop, and somehow I had icing on both of my hands as well as on the inner side of one of my elbows. "I just need to clean up." I shrugged.

"Don't forget your nose." Ellie raised an eyebrow and quirked a smile. Obviously I had frosting on my face too.

"Seriously!" I sighed. "I'll just nip upstairs." Now that I'd cleared the air with Charlotte, I felt as though a weight, one that I hadn't even realised I'd been carrying, had been lifted off my shoulders. I even forgot about my ankle as I skipped off upstairs tunelessly humming a song from the radio.

Water flowed freely from the tap while I soaped my hands, critiquing the assortment of oddities on the window sill. A huge tulip-shaped vase had been tucked into the corner. It was peculiar in that it looked as though it had been dropped at some point and the bottom had shattered, creating a crackle effect. In it stood a dark navy blue pillar candle that had never been lit. Further along was a carved fish that was roughly the same size as a melon and next to that was a much smaller wooden boat. The irony was not lost on me. Tucked into the other corner was a fishbowl-shaped vase that had been filled with a string of white fairy lights. They twinkled merrily, casting ever-changing shadows around the room even though I'd turned on the big light.

Without giving any thought to what I was doing, I reached forwards and put both my hands into the stream of water, yelped (because the water had gotten hot), and automatically pulled back. But something held me firm. The water burned as I struggled to break free from whatever had me in its grip. Panic flared inside of me. The harder I tugged, the more the water bound me in place.

"What the . . ." I started to say. The water itself was holding me where I stood. As it continued to flow over my hands, finding its way into my palms and between each of my fingers, it scalded more and more of my skin. I glanced around the room, wondering how in the hell I was going to get out of this predicament.

Glancing into the mirror, I saw my nan looking back at me. *Blake,* she whispered.

My heart pounded so hard in my chest that I feared for its ability to cope. Blood pumped ferociously through my veins, but rather than trying to calm myself, I allowed the feeling of desperation to wash over me. And then I mentally called for him, knowing that he would feel my terror. *Blake!*

Chapter 13 – Blake

Friday 19th April 2019 (Good Friday)

Blake stood off to one side of the Domplatte in Cologne, waiting for the inevitable to happen. From where he stood, he could see two of his copies, but he knew more would join their ranks sooner rather than later.

It was dusk in the German city but still, people meandered about marvelling at the twin spires of the gothic cathedral, each blackened by centuries worth of pollution. Blake had already wandered around the magnificent building himself, glancing with nothing more than a passing interest at the huge stone pillars that reached up towards the heavens, only to be capped by vaulted ceilings. While there was no denying that it was an impressive architectural feat, there were many others around the world that were equally as splendid, and he'd seen them all.

The Dom stood alone on a raised square in the centre of Cologne, some way above the river that flowed in a graceful arc through the city. People couldn't help but gravitate towards it, and as a consequence, the Domplatte was crammed full when the first gunshot was heard.

The first bullet tore through the shoulder of a middle-aged man who'd stopped on his way home to admire the view. It was impossible to see the whole of the cathedral when standing in the square. Quite frankly it was too big, and so he'd paused and looked up to the sky. The break in his usual routine was literally the death of him. The bullet pierced his skin and exploded out of his back, nicking a main artery as it continued with its flight. Acting unconsciously, the man dropped his bags and reached up to cover the wound as he fell. Blood quickly seeped between his fingers, soaking into his shirt and suit jacket before pooling on the ground. Blake knew when he'd lost his fight, he watched as a copy administered the Kiss of Death. He learned that the man was called Friedrich, that he had a wife and two boys, and that he worked as an accountant but secretly dreamed of being in a rock band.

While Blake learned all there was to know about Friedrich, absorbing those secrets that he would now be taking to the grave, he also watched the scene unfold before his eyes.

People withdrew from Friedrich, leaving him to bleed out on the pavement, unsure what was happening. A heavy silence hung in the air as people held their breath, hardly daring to move while their minds tried to grapple with the seemingly impossible . . . they were under attack. The pause did not last long, only a fraction of a second. It was hardly discernible, but Blake noticed it. He had spent centuries as a voyeur; he saw what others missed.

More shots rang out, quickly followed by the first of the screams. Interestingly those that were hit rarely made much sound. As pain washed over their bodies, radiating outwards from the source of their injuries, they either grappled for their wounds or they froze, eventually falling to the floor. Those that had not been hit, however, filled their lungs with air and bellowed as loudly as they possibly could.

People ran in all directions, but Blake didn't move; he simply stood and calmly watched the calamity. He was the first to notice the gunman, randomly firing in all directions, targeting no one and everyone. Three people were killed outright from the first set of six bullets, and in the brief interlude while the shooter reloaded, another slipped away. As well as Friedrich, a young Spanish girl and her elderly companion lost their lives. They were followed by a second German businessman. As their souls settled within Blake, he saw the life that each had lived. He learned that Ana (the Spanish girl) was vacationing with her aunt, Sofia. They'd decided to tour Germany, visiting first Cologne and then the Black Forest region of Bavaria before heading to Berlin, where Sofia had friends. Naturally they'd not planned on being gunned down while on holiday. Christian (the businessman) was older than he looked. He ran five miles every morning along the bank of the river Rhine to keep fit and played squash every weekend with his partner. In his jacket pocket he carried a ring with which he'd been planning to propose.

Blake ignored all those that died, choosing instead to focus on the gunman: a slight, Nordic-looking figure dressed from head to toe in black. She was tall with long blonde hair that was tied at the nape of her neck. Blake could sense that her death was imminent, but he didn't bother to ascertain how she would die, trusting that he'd witness it for himself in mere moments. She wore faded jeans that were ripped at each knee, a misshapen T-shirt, a cardigan that was frayed at the cuffs, and a skull cap on her head that was pulled down so far over her forehead it almost covered her pale blue eyes. She brandished the pistol as though she were afraid of it but fired confidently enough.

"Der Teufel hat mich gezwungen!" *The Devil made me.* She fired.

"Ich bin sein werkzeug!" *I am his weapon.* She fired again.

"Nur blut kann die welt reinigen!" *Only blood can cleanse the earth.* Another shot rang out.

"Ich bin verloren!" *I am forsaken.* Click. Click. Click. The gun didn't go off. A puzzled look crossed her face, and she raised the gun to her eye to look down its barrel.

"Lass seinen willen geschehen!" *Let his will be made clear.* Her last words rang out clearly enough despite the chaos that swirled around her. Without taking the gun away from her eye, she pulled the trigger one last time. This time the bullet flew from its chamber, passing through her eye as though it was nothing more than a vacant space, ripping apart brain cells, and exploding out of the back of her skull before finally embedding itself in a wall on the other side of the street. Her death was near instantaneous; one of Blake's copies had attended to her even before her body had settled on the pavement.

What surprised Blake the most was that her soul had not turned the colour of soot. There wasn't even a hint of black or staining to be seen. Heidi was a good person driven by lunacy to do a horrible thing. The voices had started when she'd been young, but she'd been able to ignore them until she was much older, and only when she was visited by a demon did her precious sanity finally fracture, shattering into a million small pieces. She'd been prescribed various medications over the years and had spent time in facilities, but nothing had really helped. Her last thought had been one of peace.

Blake had always dismissed sightings of anything demonic as nothing more than flights of fantasy, but after everything he'd learned recently, he was starting to wonder. Perhaps those who were afflicted with hallucinogenic disorders such as schizophrenia had been ambushed by beings from hell. Lost in thought as he was, he barely noticed the last lives that were lost. Not even the flashing blue lights of the polizei were able to intrude on his thoughts. But Emma's panic did; her terror roused him from his deliberations, slicing through him like a hot knife carving through cold butter.

Blake! she screamed in the silence of his mind. Through her eyes, he saw her reflection. Sweat beaded her forehead and tears rolled down her cheeks. All of her usual colour had been washed from her face making her freckles more pronounced than usual. Blake had never seen the world through her eyes, but now was not the time to marvel at whatever was happening. Without giving another thought to the tragedy in Cologne, he translocated to where Emma was.

"The water," she gasped. "Blake, quickly."

Blake acted on instinct. He reached into the ether and retrieved his weapon. There was limited space in the bathroom, but reality had never hampered his abilities before. He swung the scythe in the general direction of the enchanted water. The blade sliced through both the metal tap and the porcelain bowl, severing the liquid stream from its source. Droplets of the scorching hot water fell from Emma's hands and arms, splashing harmlessly onto the floor and hissing as they rapidly cooled against the tiles. Blake felt an evil awareness fill the room. An inexplicable pressure started to build in the air; he turned to shield Emma's body just as an explosion tore apart the bathroom. With Emma cradled in his arms, he was thrown backwards, through the door, landing at the top of the stairs. Charlotte's entire bathroom looked like a bomb had been dropped on it.

Chapter 14 – Ellie

Friday 19th April 2019 (Good Friday)

Ellie had just bitten into a mushroom filled vol-au-vent when the detonation sounded upstairs. The crunch of the puff pastry paired beautifully with the creamy filling, but it was forgotten in an instant. She turned on instinct, dropping the half-eaten food to the floor, and sprinted up the stairs to where Emma was, moving faster than had been possible before Abaddon had gifted her with 'an edge.' All Charlotte, Rhona, Angela, and Tori saw was a blur as she sped from the room. Their reactions were more normal: they flinched and dropped into a half crouch because while the primitive half of their brains screamed at them to run, the logical half scoffed at their innate desire to escape. The result was that each of the four women stared gormlessly at each other in shock, stunned into silence.

Clouds of dust greeted Ellie at the top of the stairs. Blake lay on top of Emma, his heavy body covering most of hers. All Ellie could see of Emma was a sliver of her copper-coloured locks and one of her arms.

The bathroom looked like a disaster zone. The bath and the toilet were still standing in situ, but the sink had been cleaved in two. A tiny portion of it (along with a single solitary tap) remained clinging to the wall, grimly holding on for dear life, but the rest of it had given in to gravity and fallen, shattering into hundreds of pieces when it had hit the floor. It now lay strewn across the tiles, broken into jagged chunks of porcelain. Water seeped from somewhere, gathering the cement dust into a sticky gooey mess.

"Emma!" Ellie gasped. "Blake, what happened?"

Blake started to answer, lifting himself from Emma, but Ellie interrupted. "No, don't, get out of here. I can find a way to explain this but not you."

Blake started to protest but was cut off again. "It's okay, Blake," Emma mumbled, her words slurred. It sounded as though she'd just woken from a deep sleep. "Go."

Ellie let out a breath that she hadn't realised she'd been holding while Blake did as he was told, blinking out of sight just before Charlotte appeared.

"What on earth . . ." she asked, her word trailing off as she surveyed the scene.

"Charlotte," Ellie spoke authoritatively. "I need you to turn off the water and get one of the others to ring 9-9-9."

"What caused this?"

"I don't know, a gas leak maybe," Ellie answered. Wasn't the answer always a gas leak when something unexplainable needed explaining away? "Go turn off the water and ring 9-9-9. Emma's been hurt."

Charlotte turned without argument or comment and padded away. Her wide-legged, black trousers, white blouse and pink, sparkly flats were all covered in a greyish-coloured powder by the time she reached the bottom of the stairs.

Ellie sat down beside Emma, not caring about her own clothes, and took Emma's hand in her own. There was no denying that Emma was bigger than her, but somehow she seemed so small and broken in that moment. "What the hell happened?" she asked.

Emma coughed; she'd evidently inhaled a serious amount of the ick that now floated lazily in the air. "It was the water," she answered. Her voice was hoarse, but her breathing sounded even and regular. She tried to pull herself into a seated position, but Ellie stopped her, gently laying a hand on her chest.

"Don't. You'd best stay where you are in case you've broken something. An ambulance is on its way."

"I don't need an ambulance," Emma argued, still struggling to get up.

"Emma, for all I know you have a concussion, and what the hell are those burn marks on your wrists; they're blistering already."

Emma slumped back, the fight draining from her. "I told you, it was the water."

"That doesn't even begin to make sense," Ellie replied.

"None of this makes any sense," Emma muttered, her eyes closing. Ellie knew that if she wasn't in so much pain, her words would have had much more of a cynical edge. Emma couldn't help but wrap herself in a cloak of sarcasm; it was how she dealt with her insecurities. Emma believed she was too tall, too big, too fat, too everything. She'd grown up in a normal loving family in exactly the same way that Ellie had, but for some reason, she was plagued with doubt in a way that Ellie didn't fully comprehend.

"Hey, hey! No going to sleep," Ellie barked, channelling her inner Emma and snapping her fingers in front of Emma's eyes, breathing a sigh of relief when they opened a crack. Emma raised an eyebrow at Ellie but otherwise didn't respond. *That's got to be a good sign, right?* she thought. "You have to stay awake until the paramedics get here."

"Because . . .?"

"Because that's what they say in all the movies."

"Uh-huh. Tell me about Scott then. Keep me awake."

"You know all about Scott; he's your brother."

"But you're the one who's in love with him."

"Am I? Methinks you are abusing your position somewhat." Ellie couldn't help but chuckle despite the gravity of the situation.

Emma shrugged slightly. "Maybe."

"When did you know you were in love with Blake?" Ellie deftly deflected the spotlight from herself onto Emma, who either didn't notice or wasn't bothered.

"Who says I'm in love with him?"

"Come on, Emma. When are you going to admit it to yourself?"

"Fine. The first night we met, when he slapped me," she answered wearily, not having the energy to argue the toss.

"When he slapped you?" It was Ellie's turn to raise her eyebrows.

"Yes. I didn't realise it at the time, but I've been thinking about it ever since you . . ." Emma paused and started to cough.

"Ever since I what, Emma?"

"Ever since you pointed out that he'd moved in with me."

Ellie raised an eyebrow. "Really? You needed me to point that out to you?"

"Apparently so." Emma coughed some more.

Ellie looked on, concerned but unsure what more to do. "We shouldn't have come tonight, should we?"

"Ellie, listen to me. This is not your fault. I don't know what the hell is going on, but I do know that it's not your fault. Even what your mum did is not your fault."

Ellie flinched and glanced away.

"Ellie, promise me that you don't blame yourself for any of this."

"I can't do that."

Emma could barely make out what Ellie had said, she'd spoken so quietly. "Not. Your. Fault," she reiterated, as firmly as possible, but her voice was getting increasingly hoarse.

"You didn't even want to come."

"No, I didn't. But you did. And Blake didn't sense anything untoward happening, nothing that would result in my death anyway, so we may as well start assuming now that I'm going to survive the night." A shiver ran through her body and she started coughing again.

"Do you want anything?" Ellie asked, changing the subject.

"Some water would be good," Emma replied, barely managing to get the words out. Her throat was so dry, swallowing a razor blade would have been an easier feat.

"Hey!" Ellie twisted her body and shouted down the stairs. "Can one of you guys pass me up some water?"

It was Tori who brought up a bottle. "Hey you," she said to Emma, smiling despite the mask of worry that clouded her face, before addressing Ellie. "Charlotte's waiting outside for the ambulance," she remarked. "We're staying out of the way, but we're here if you need us," she finished before retreating back down the stairs.

"Thanks," Ellie replied to Tori before helping Emma to have a drink. "So, what was it about that slap that got you all hot and bothered for Mr. Tall, Dark, and Handsome? I didn't think you'd be into anything kinky," she prompted when Tori was safely out of earshot.

Emma rolled her eyes as best she could before answering. "It made me feel whole for the first time in my life. I don't really know how to describe it, but a sense of peace stole over me. All of my life I've felt on edge, almost irritable, but when Blake did what he did, something changed inside of me. I felt in alignment for the first time ever. I didn't even know that anything was wrong with me until then."

"There's nothing wrong with you."

"You know what I mean."

Ellie let Emma's comment pass. "I guess you couldn't help but be in love with Blake; you are his soulmate after all."

"Not technically."

"Don't you start. Blake is enough of a pedant, thank you very much."

Emma smiled briefly. "Maybe that's why we're drawn together."

"Maybe. But you also like him, right?"

"Of course. I know he can be a pain in the rear end, but if I'd been alone for almost a thousand years, I'm sure I'd be exactly the same. Anyway, why do you ask? Was it just to keep me talking?"

"Partly. But partly because I've never had a moment with Scott. I do love him, but we've never bonded like that."

"Ellie, you goose! You've grown up with Scott. You've been in love with him from before you could speak. You probably had your moment when you were about three!"

"I don't know . . ."

"Ellie, look at me. Hey! I might be dying. Look at me."

"You're not dying." Ellie laughed, shaking her head. "Are you? Do you think you should check in with Blake? You said you weren't a moment ago."

"We're all dying. Every breath we take is one closer to our last one."

"That's a bit deep, considering the circumstances we find ourselves in. What did Blake say? I assume he's close by still."

"He's busy berating himself for leaving me alone tonight."

"You can hear his thoughts now?"

"No, but I'm drowning in his guilt. Anyway, stop trying to change the subject. I want you to know that it's okay for you to be in love with Scott, regardless of whether or not you've had a moment. Love's different for us all."

"But he's your brother," Ellie argued.

"So?"

"What if I pursued a relationship and it went wrong?"

"What if it didn't?" Emma countered.

Ellie—queen of the witty one-liners—couldn't think of anything to say to that. Instead she squeezed Emma's hand tightly in her own. Silence fell over the two girls, but it was a comfortable one. They'd been best friends for so long that they didn't need to fill every second with inane chatter.

Chapter 15 – Emma

Saturday 20th April 2019

Despite the last few hours being traumatic enough to give me nightmares, I was desperate for some rest. However, sleep eluded me. The problem was that hospitals were never really quiet, and I jumped at every other sound. The ward I'd been transferred to for observation after being checked out in A&E was a general one, so there remained a degree of hustle and bustle despite it being after midnight. Some patients slept soundly, blissfully ignorant to the fact that their snoring was keeping everyone else awake, while others tossed and turned, moaning and groaning. Nurses moved between patients checking vital signs and machines beeped cheerily away to themselves in the background.

"Why couldn't I have just gone home?" I muttered to myself, fidgeting around in my bed, trying to persuade my body to give up its fight and go to sleep.

Because the doctor said you had to stay, Blake answered even though my question had been A) rhetorical, and B) really only intended for my ears. Blake had adamantly refused to leave the hospital grounds after I'd been admitted; however, he had been persuaded to remain outside of my bubble. I couldn't actually see him from where I lay, propped up in that peculiar half seated position that's only possible in a hospital bed, but I knew he was somewhere close by, and if I'm being honest about it, I was comforted by that fact. Obviously I wasn't so comforted that I was able to fall into a deep and dreamless slumber, but I was comforted nonetheless.

After the paramedics had arrived at Charlotte's house (poor Charlotte, I didn't know how I was going to explain away what had happened to her bathroom) and whisked me away for treatment, it dawned on me just how much my whole body ached. The burns on my wrists (now coated in some kind of weird paste and bandaged for protection) were painful and . . . well, they burned. Quite simply there was no other word for it. My back felt bruised and sore, and my joints were tender. The ambulance ride, though, had been relatively pleasant, in so much as I'd felt like I'd been driven to my death in a stuffy hearse with the Angel of Death hovering over me, because Blake had literally ridden to the hospital on the roof of the ambulance, and I could sense his heated emotions throughout the entire journey. Idly I'd wondered if my bubble had ever forced him to manifest while he'd been up there, but he hadn't said. That would have been some show, hey?

Ellie, her parents (yes, even Joanne, who'd seemed oddly distressed by what had happened to me), my parents, and Scott had all raced to Blackpool Vic to be by my side, and I'd been delighted to see Ellie sneaking her hand into my brother's bear claw of a mitt. That almost made the agony worthwhile. Almost. Next time I had to persuade my best friend to accept that she was in love with my brother, I was going to have to find another way to make sure she was listening to me. Oh wait! There wasn't going to be a next time. I only had one best friend and one brother. Wedding bells, interspersed with snippets of 'Time to Say Goodbye,' had played in a loop in my head since that moment.

All of my visitors had been shooed out of the building by a particularly firm ward sister some time ago and since then I'd been on my own, first of all staring at the ceiling in A&E before ending up on Ward 29.

Frustrated, and unable to stay in bed for a moment longer, I threw back the covers, sat up, and turned so that I could hang my legs off the side of the bed.

Where are you going? Blake demanded to know.

I'm going for a wee, I snapped, a little more waspishly than I'd intended.

My mum had had the foresight to bring some pyjamas and a pair of slippers with her when she'd got the call from Ellie. I hadn't really gotten to the bottom of why she'd assumed I'd be staying in hospital overnight, but my mum was Mrs. Pragmatic. She'd probably packed them 'just in case,' as was her way. Whatever her rationale, I was immensely grateful that I didn't have to suffer the humiliation of tottering to the bathroom wearing one of those gowns that opened at the back. My bottom was not intended for general viewing and the underwear I'd worn to Charlotte's party didn't leave much to the imagination. Mum's pyjamas weren't exactly my preferred style, but they were better than nothing.

Slowly, and feeling like I was well over eighty years old, I shuffled off in the direction of the bathroom. I didn't really need a wee, but I half hoped that by doing one, my body would magically reset itself and sleep would then welcome me with open arms.

"Are you okay, love?" one of the staff asked as I passed the dimly lit nurse's station.

"Yes, thanks. I just need the bathroom," I answered politely with a smile on my face even though what I wanted to say was: *No, I'm not okay. Quite frankly my wrists and arms hurt like a bitch and I feel like I've been used as a punching bag by someone much bigger and heavier than I am. And don't even get me started on all the random crap that's happening in my life at the minute. We'll gloss over the fact that my best friend's mum tried to kill me and focus on the fact that I've been attacked by the wind and then held hostage by scorching hot water. Am I okay? No! No, I'm bloody well not okay!*

Toilets in hospitals looked the same the whole world over. The room was quite big and square (well, quite frankly compared to my bathroom at home, it was palatial; wheelchair-friendly, I assumed) with a bright red pull cord next to the loo, a sink in the corner, and a mirror on the wall. I didn't bother to look in the mirror before lowering my shorts and gingerly sitting down, but I did wonder about its placement. It was full length and screwed to the wall immediately opposite where I had to sit, giving me a full-frontal view when I eventually looked up.

Delightful, I thought. My hair, which had looked quite nice when I'd left for Charlotte's party, was still pinned back but was now in complete disarray. I looked like a scarecrow with bits of carrot-coloured straw glued to my head. I had dark shadows underneath my eyes that were accentuated by the remnants of my makeup (my mum might have thought to pack me some pyjamas, but she hadn't packed any facial wipes), and my skin had taken on a waxy complexion. Usually the freckles on my face served to give me some colour, but today they just looked like dirty smudges. *What does Blake see in me?* I wondered, but before he could answer, my reflection shifted into that of my nan.

Find her, she whispered to me before the image changed again.

While I was getting used to seeing any one of my ancestors in the mirror, they'd never shown me anyone else, and so it was a bit of a surprise when my nan's face blurred and became that of a young teenager, one that I'd seen before. She had the hood of her jumper pulled up over her face, but there was no doubting it was the girl I'd bumped into when I'd had my last check-up. I was blown away by her breathtaking beauty. She had exceptionally dark hair that had been pulled back into a ponytail underneath her hood. She had dark almond-shaped eyes; a long, straight nose; chiselled cheekbones; and plump rose-coloured lips.

"Find her?" I asked, seeking clarity. "I don't even know who she is, let alone where she'll be."

Where was she the last time you met her?

"She was here, but she'll have gone home by now."

Will she?

"Well, yes. Unless she's staff and happens to be on duty. She doesn't look like staff though."

Hmmm, and what about if she was dead?

"Dead?" I squeaked. "She's a ghost! Does that mean she's trapped here?"

My nan hummed in response.

"She's a ghost?" I repeated, shocked by what I was hearing. "No." I shook my head in disbelief. "She's so young."

Tragedy doesn't always strike the elderly. My nan's image replaced that of the young girl before fading away until I was sat looking at myself once more, my shorts around my ankles, my feet wedged into an old pair of slippers that were, in reality, a soupçon too small for me.

I finished what I'd sat down to do, stood and sorted myself out, flushed, washed up, and then exited the bathroom, lost in thought. That girl, the one that had walked into me when I'd arbitrarily stopped dead en-route to an appointment in this very hospital, had been a ghost. But if she'd been a ghost, how had she collided with me? She'd looked exactly like a real live girl to me. I'd even spoken to her and she'd replied. I remembered back to that day, back to the conversation Ellie and I had had about ghosts. Had I always been able to see them? Was that even a possibility? I'd never believed in the supernatural until I'd met Blake, so it wouldn't have ever entered my head to assume anything odd.

Blake? I asked.

Yes.

I take it you got all of that?

Yes.

I'm going to go and see if I can find her.

She's not lost.

What do you mean?

She's in the corridor downstairs at the minute.

Is she?

Yes, but I wouldn't bother. She'll avoid you.

Why?

Because all remnants avoid me.

That doesn't mean she will me.

It's likely though.

Hmm . . . why do they avoid you again?

I don't know. A surge of emotion washed over me, but it wasn't one of my own. Blake had spent many centuries alone, and he'd been hurt and frustrated when he'd realised that ghosts avoided him. Dark clouds of betrayal and dismay, interspersed with brief glimpses of Blake approaching first one person, and then a second and a third only to have all of them disappear, filtered into my consciousness.

What's happening? I asked, bewildered.

You're seeing my thoughts, Blake answered dryly.

A cacophony of mixed feelings swelled inside of me. A part of me felt like a child on orange juice. At last! Blake had been able to hear my every thought (as long as he was within range) ever since we'd known each other, but I'd never had a peep out of him. I'd been desperate to turn the tables! But at the same time, my knees almost buckled with the weight of the immense pain that Blake had endured throughout his life. While half of me was giddy with delight and wanted to dance around a maypole (or just wiggle about comically where I stood) because I was finally able to read him in a way that I'd started to think was impossible, half of me was overwhelmed with the desolation that Blake had suffered and wanted nothing more than to sink into the depths of despair. The word 'grief' just didn't cut it. He'd been so alone, so lonely. His whole life had been devoid of company. But for him, his whole life wasn't just a number of decades, it was centuries.

I do not want your pity, Blake snapped at me, jolting me out of my thoughts.

I don't pity you, Blake; I feel empathy for what you've suffered.

Blake did not reply. His emotions were now mixed with overtones of anger and annoyance.

I know you don't have all that much experience with human emotion, but trust me when I tell you that there's a difference between pity and empathy. Anyway, maybe I can solve the mystery of the remnants for us. I used his preferred term in a conscious attempt to mollify him. *Why do you think my nan wants me to find her? Am I supposed to help her, or is she supposed to help me?*

Maybe both.

Maybe. Do you think this is a good idea?

No. That was Blake to a tee; why waste words when one will do?

But you won't try and stop me?

I won't.

Okay, let's do this then.

While Blake and I had been chatting, I'd drifted into a common room that I'd found so I could stand and stare out of the window, not that there was a great deal to see. Hospital buildings were laid out in front of me, but in the gloom of night, I could barely work out where I was in relation to the major landmarks that Blackpool was famous for, namely its tower and the seafront. Taking a deep breath, I turned and marched directly to the door that cut the ward off from the hustle and bustle of the rest of the hospital.

"And just where do you think you're going?" A jovial but firm voice sounded behind me just as I reached for the handle, reminding me I was a patient and therefore not exactly free to come and go as I pleased.

I turned and saw that it was the same member of staff who'd asked if I was okay, an older man with a shock of ginger hair, a matching beard, and a bit of a paunch. He looked friendly enough, with a broad grin and a twinkle in his eye. "Erm, I thought I'd go for a walk," I replied, innocently enough.

"I can't really let you off the ward now, can I?" He continued to smile at me. I felt like a five-year-old being reprimanded by a redheaded Santa Claus dressed up like a nurse. He wasn't actually that fat, but once the idea was in my head, I just couldn't shake it.

"Pleeeaaaassseeee," I wheedled, using my best little-girl-lost voice, working on the assumption that as it had never failed to disarm my dad it wouldn't fail me now. I even looked up at him from underneath my eyelashes, wrung my hands together, and fidgeted on the spot, but Mr. Jovial just laughed and shook his head.

"Come on, if you can't sleep, by all means sit in the common room, but until you're discharged, I'm not letting you out of my sight." He paused briefly, giving me hope but then dashed them by adding, "I tell you what I'll do, though, I'll rustle you up a cup of tea and a biscuit. I think we've got a packet of chocolate digestives knocking around here somewhere."

I pulled a face, not because of the choice of biscuit I'd been offered but because I really wanted off the ward. Mr. Jovial (I really needed to work out his name, but the badge that dangled on a lanyard around his neck was currently facing backwards), however, assumed otherwise.

"Don't like digestives, hey?"

"I'm more of a hobnob girl, actually," I answered without thinking, instead wondering how the hell I was going to break myself out of the prison I'd found myself in. I was just starting to wonder if I could discharge myself when my jailer unwittingly gave me the answer.

"They do have those in the vending machines downstairs . . ." His voice trailed off.

"Really? Perhaps I could just nip down and get some? Maybe? I am famished." Hope swelled inside of me.

"You're not going to let this drop, are you?"

"Not a chance. But I promise to go straight to the vending machine and then come right back." I grinned.

"Go on then, seeing as how you've decided to act like an adult instead of a little child. You've got ten minutes."

"Fifteen," I bartered. "I recently broke my ankle; I'm a slow walker at the minute."

"Hmmm, I saw that in your notes. Okay then, fifteen. The clock starts now."

I didn't need telling twice; I was out of the door in a heartbeat. I'd have liked to have sprinted to where I thought Casper (my hopefully friendly ghost) might be despite the fact that my ankle was genuinely still recovering, but two things held me back. Firstly, I was still in a degree of pain, even though I'd taken my meds, and secondly, the Vic was only part hospital. It was also part rabbit warren. I followed the signs for the main entrance, assuming they would eventually spit me out onto my favourite corridor in all the land.

In the end it only took me a couple minutes to find my way down to the ground floor, but then I had to find *her*. The last time I'd met her, when I hadn't even known she was a ghost, *she'd* bumped into *me*, so I didn't really know where to start looking. I hadn't exactly thought this one through. In fact, if you'd have pressed me before I'd set off on my exciting adventure, I'd have probably said something like, *It'll be fine, she'll be there.* See, I could be eloquent!

Dammit, where is she? I muttered in the silence of my own mind, half expecting Blake to point me in the right direction bearing in mind he'd confirmed her as being here not that long ago, but he didn't.

Not having much to go on and not having much time, I set off walking up the corridor and then stopped suddenly, hoping she'd bump into me like last time. Nothing happened. Maybe I'd gone in the wrong direction. I turned on heel and then set off walking in the other direction before coming to an abrupt halt. Still nothing happened. I tried to remember exactly where I'd been when we'd met, but the whole corridor looked like one long unending sea of pale green painted brickwork interspersed with framed pictures of Blackpool in times gone past.

After about five minutes of repeatedly walking ten or fifteen yards and then stopping abruptly, I was getting hot and bothered, despite only wearing a pair of my mum's cotton pyjamas and some old slippers. I sighed loudly and leaned against the wall, resting my bottom as comfortably as I could and leaning my torso forwards, propping myself up by securing my hands on my thighs.

At least there's no one around to see me behaving like a lunatic, I thought, grateful that I was alone. Or so I thought.

"What are you doing?" a female voice asked.

I stood up straight and found myself almost nose to nose with the girl I'd been looking for.

"You!" I exclaimed delighted. "Shit, I really need to get back to the ward now. Will you come with me?"

She looked at me quizzically, her brow furrowed. "What were you doing?" she asked again, changing the tense. Previously I'd thought her distressed because of the way she'd rasped the only word she'd ever spoken to me—s'okay. However, all traces of her sorrow had vanished. Instead, she seemed as bright as a button, albeit her voice retained its husky quality.

"I was looking for you." I thought that was a given, but maybe it was only obvious to me because I knew what I'd been up to.

"Why?"

"To be honest, I was told to find you. Listen, please, will you come with me? Back to the ward? They'll send a search party if I'm not back soon, but I really want to talk to you."

"Why didn't you just call my name then?"

"I don't even know your name," I answered honestly while wondering how in hell I was going to move her along and get her upstairs with me. Ghosts, it seemed, had a different perspective on time than us mere mortals.

"It's Jennifer," she replied, turning her head slightly to stare absently over my shoulder, making me think of Cooper and Watson. It creeped me out when they did it too.

"Jennifer." I smiled as brightly as I could. "So, will you . . . come with me?"

"Why should I?"

"Erm . . ." I guessed 'because I asked you to' wasn't going to cut it, but I couldn't really think of any other explanation to offer up.

"Maybe if you tell me your name, I'll consider it," Jennifer prompted.

"Goodness, where are my manners? Of course." I laughed, although even I heard how fake my little titter sounded. *Moving swiftly on,* I admonished myself. "I'm Emma. It's lovely to meet you."

I held out my hand to shake hers, but Jennifer ignored it. "We've met before. Twice," she said.

"Have we? I thought we'd only met once."

"No." Jennifer didn't elaborate, and a sharp sense of frustration curled around my abdomen.

"Listen, I really have got to get back upstairs. Please meet me there. Ward 29."

"Okay," Jennifer answered and then pulled a Blake by simply disappearing on me.

I didn't know what I'd said to gain her agreement, but I didn't want to waste her goodwill by making her wait for me. "That's just annoying," I muttered out loud to myself.

At least she didn't avoid you, Blake answered.

I guess. She was a bit vague, though, wasn't she?

Maybe all remnants are like that.

Hmmm, maybe, I replied, turning around and setting off back towards the ward. Now all I had to do was find my way back through the maze to my bed and my belongings.

Chapter 16 – Emma

Saturday 20th April 2019

"Jennifer?" I asked the empty common room some time later after being suitably admonished by Mr. Jovial when I'd eventually retraced my steps and found where I was meant to be. He'd seemed more concerned about the fact that the tea he'd made me had started to go cold rather than the fact I'd been twenty minutes and not our agreed fifteen though. I was starting to think Mr. Jovial was actually quite the sweetie.

"Yes," Jennifer replied from the doorway.

I exhaled loudly, releasing a breath I hadn't even realised I'd been holding, and let myself drop into the seat nearest me. "You came."

"I don't tend to bother with the wards," she remarked, but I got the distinct impression that she was talking to herself and not to me. She wandered around, inspecting all and sundry. Personally, I didn't think the room was all that interesting. I mean, let's be honest here, it was a fairly bland, square-ish shaped room filled with those plastic-coated, upright chairs favoured by care facilities. The only point of interest (in my mind) was the television that was screwed to the wall in one of the far corners. While she drifted from point to point, I studied her intently. She was still dressed as she'd been the other day—'boyfriend' jeans, an oversized hoodie, and a pair of scuffed trainers. The jeans were dark blue with a rip at the knee, the hoodie was plain black with a small orange logo on the left-hand shoulder, and the trainers were those that were tipped white, not that they looked white anymore. Her hood was still pulled up over her face, but now that I had the time to watch her, it was possible to discern just how stunning she was. She was radiant, except for the haunted look and the bruise-like shadows underneath her eyes.

"What happened to you?" I blurted out, without thinking about what I was asking or the fact that she might not want to answer such questions.

"Aren't you worried about what this looks like?"

"What what looks like?" I was puzzled. Jennifer had a talent for turning our conversation on its head.

"This. You do know that you look like you're talking to the wall, don't you?"

"Do I?"

"Well d'oh, no one else can see me. I am dead after all."

The thought hadn't occurred actually but seeing as it was awful 'o' clock in the morning and with the exception of a handful of staff most people were tucked up in their beds, I decided not to worry about it. "Why? How did you die? And why are you still here?" Etiquette had evidently left the building. The fact that I was asking some sensitive questions didn't even enter my head. Ghosts were real. And not only were they a thing, I could see them. In fact, I was sitting having a conversation with one. Talk about being mind-blown. Even though I'd recently learned that the Grim Reaper was a sentient being and not just the stuff of myth and legend, the supernatural world still managed to surprise me.

Jennifer, who hadn't yet bothered with a seat, stilled for a moment before glancing briefly in my direction and then looking away. I wondered if I'd made a mistake by asking such blunt questions, but after a minute or two, she finally answered. "It was my mum. She wasn't very well. She suffocated me in my bed one night and then slit her own wrists. When He came and took my soul she was still alive, so I stayed put. I wanted to make sure that she was treated right, so I stayed with her. My dad found us and called an ambulance. I rode with her all the way here, and I've been here ever since."

"Oh Jenny, that's awful." My heart bled for this poor girl. I couldn't imagine anything worse happening to her. No wonder she looked like a victim . . . she was. I'd assumed she'd died because of an illness or maybe a car accident, but this! This was terrible.

"It's Jennifer," she declared hotly, interrupting my thoughts.

"I'm sorry," I replied quickly, biting my lip and praying that she wouldn't disappear on me. "So, is your mum here too?"

Jennifer turned to look properly at me, her face twisted into a frown. "Why would she be here?"

"Didn't she stay too? To be with you?"

"No, she was sent to a secure unit."

"She lived?"

"Yes, the doctors got to her in time. But here I am, stuck."

"And you forgave her for what she did to you?"

"Of course I forgave her. She was ill," Jennifer spat, her voice full of heat and passion but also an underlying tone of sorrow. She clearly loved her mum, despite what she'd done to her, but I suspected that she also felt a degree of resentment.

"Jennifer, I'm so sorry. I really don't know what to say." It was impossible not to sympathise with her. Only a monster would feel nothing for the scruffy-looking urchin standing in front of me.

"You could tell me what you want?"

If only I knew, I thought. "Erm, well . . ." I paused, not really knowing what to say. My nan had not exactly been explicit as to why I needed to find Jennifer. Was it for my benefit or for hers? Was she meant to help me with something, and if so, what? Or was I meant to help her with something? Maybe I was meant to help her find peace? But why her? Why not anyone else? I knew for a fact that Jennifer wasn't the only ghost in the hospital because on the day I'd bumped into her, I'd also seen a man who looked like he'd walked straight out of the '50s.

"Well?"

"So, here's the thing," I started. "I have a bit of a strange connection with my ancestors. Sometimes I see one of their reflections in place of my own, and sometimes they tell me things."

"Really? Is that because of your connection with *him*?" Intrigue was evident in how Jennifer spoke. She finally took a seat, although she didn't relax into it. She perched with one knee crossed over the other, one arm tucked around her slender waist and one arm forming a prop for her to rest her chin on.

"You know about that?"

"Yes."

"How?"

"Someone told me. You shine golden like he does, but you're much more powerful." She smiled then, only faintly, but for a brief moment, I glimpsed the girl that she might have been if only she'd lived.

"I do? I am?" How was I only just hearing about this? Why the hell hadn't Blake told me before that I was part glow-worm?

"You do to me."

"So what? Do I look like the sun or something? And what do you mean by 'more powerful'? I can't do anything. I'm just a normal girl."

She stood and leaned into me, whispering very quietly into my ear, "You are the Key. You can control everything he does."

"What? I don't understand. How can I shine? Wha—"

It's your soul, Blake supplied. *Remnants must be able to see them. Ask her if she can see everyone's or just yours,* he prompted, not that Jennifer gave me the chance.

She sat back down and sighed mournfully. "I miss the sun," she said, not even attempting to answer my questions.

"Are you literally stuck here? Can't you leave?" I asked. I wanted to grill her about what she'd whispered in my ear, but I knew I'd lost her.

"I can, but I don't."

"Why would you stay here when you can go anywhere you want?"

"It's the compulsion."

"What compulsion?" I asked sharply. Jennifer was starting to irritate me. Of course I felt for her, but did she have to be so flipping abstract all the time?

"It's the same for all of us. We're compelled to stay in one place."

"Huh." My annoyance was washed away by a surge of compassion. Not only had she had one of the most wretched deaths imaginable, she was also a pseudo prisoner in the afterlife. Maybe my nan had wanted me to find her so that I could help her instead of the reverse. "Why here? Why not where you died?"

Jennifer didn't even pretend to answer my question. "Why are you here?" she asked, putting the focus back onto me.

While I wanted to roll my eyes, I decided it would be easier just to answer her question. "I don't even know how to explain it, to be honest," I started. "I was washing my hands when the water attacked me."

"It what?"

"The water held me fast and burned me. See?" I held out my hands, palm upwards, so that she could see the bandages wrapped around my wrists.

Jennifer stood and stepped closer to me, taking hold of my hands and turning them over to inspect them closely even though they were bandaged. Her skin was icy to the touch, and an involuntary shiver ran through my body. "You're freezing," I stated, not really expecting a response.

"Dead," Jennifer helpfully supplied as though that explained it. Perhaps it did? For all I knew, all ghosts were chilly. Maybe a ghost was behind every cold spot in the whole of the world. "Are you being haunted?" Jennifer dropped my hands and took a step away from me, almost as though I was shrouded in a bad smell.

"Why would you think that?"

"Spirits can control the elements."

"Can they?"

Jennifer shrugged nonchalantly, returning to her seat. "I can; I assume the others can too. I tend not to bother though."

"By 'control the elements,' just what do you mean exactly?" My mind had woken up and was busy adding two and two together. But was it coming up with three, four, or five as an answer? Only some of the weird and crazy crap that had been happening to me could be explained by what Jennifer had referred to as 'a haunting.' The fire at The Sparrowhawk . . . Blake had said it was unnatural . . . the peculiar wind monster . . . the water . . . but not the blood on my door. And Blake had previously dismissed the notion.

Blake, are you hearing this? You said that ghosts didn't hurt people.

They don't.

But maybe one does.

Before Blake could answer, Jennifer interrupted. "Are you speaking to him?"

"I was. How could you tell?"

"I've had a lot of practice reading body language. There isn't much else to do in the afterlife, you know. I mostly watch people. Is he coming here?"

"I'm sure he could if you wanted him to."

"I don't." An involuntary shudder made her twitch slightly. Her hatred of Blake was almost palpable in the air.

"Okay, I'll make sure he stays away then," I quickly reassured, not wanting anything to upset her. Our conversation was providing me with a number of valuable little snippets of information. "Why don't you like him? He wasn't responsible for your death, you know?"

"I know."

"So, why don't you like him?" I pushed her for something more than she was willing to offer up voluntarily.

Jennifer glared at me but eventually gave me a small crumb of information to work with. "I don't want to be sent away."

"Why would he do that?" I was genuinely puzzled by her response. I'd expected her to say that she blamed him for her death or that she didn't like him because he'd taken her soul. What I didn't expect was her to be fearful of him dismissing her.

"I don't know why he would want to do it; I just know he could if he chose to."

"He could?" What was Jennifer trying to tell me? That Blake could compel the dead to do as he wished? And where would he send them? Heaven? Hell? That didn't really align with what Abaddon had had to say about the other dimensions.

"Don't you know anything?"

Jennifer's sarcasm wound me up in an instant, even though I used it on a regular basis myself. The last three months hadn't exactly been the best in my life, even though I'd met the love of my life during that time. My own infamous anger made itself known as a spike of fury shot through me. "Quite frankly, no, I don't. I haven't had years and years to research what it means to be soulmates with him. Until recently I didn't even know he existed. And ghosts such as yourselves . . . only a few weeks ago I'd have laughed if you'd have suggested I'd be having a conversation with one. Excuse me for being ignorant. I haven't yet had the time to sign on at the School for Supernatural Dummies, what with losing Grammy, being stalked by a madman, and spending weeks recovering only to find myself effectively housebound because every time I set foot outside, I get attacked by a gale."

"Better?" Jennifer asked, an eyebrow raised. She suddenly looked much older than I was, making me wonder about her age, both in terms of when she'd died and how many years she'd roamed the corridors of the Vic.

"Yes," I answered honestly, breathing a sigh of relief because surprisingly I did feel better. Ever since that night—the one where Peter Collins had made himself known—I'd felt on edge, unable to let go, unable to relax. Don't get me wrong, I'd repeatedly said I was fine. I'd even believed it, but in the back of my mind, there'd always been a persistent itch, an annoying, irritating sense that there was something wrong. I'd never even acknowledged it to myself, let alone talked to anyone about it. No doubt Blake had felt it, although he'd never pushed me on it, and I was absolutely certain that Ellie had spotted it based on some of her comments. Somehow, though, I'd missed it. The human mind is remarkably talented at hiding the truth from itself. I'd jumped at loud noises and laughed it off as being silly, I'd checked and double-checked that the door was locked and told myself that that was normal. I'd even looked under the bed before snuggling down for the night and reassured myself that that was sensible.

Blake, why didn't you say something? I asked, undecided if I was hurt by his inattention or grateful that he hadn't pointed out what should have been obvious.

You weren't ready to talk about it, he replied.

While I processed what had just become apparent to me, Jennifer sat quietly, seemingly content to let time slide by. Eventually I gave myself a little shake and spoke up. "I don't know for definite why my nan pointed me in your direction, but you've helped me in ways that I hadn't even imagined possible because I didn't know I needed helping. Is there anything I can do for you? Don't you want to leave here? Move on?" I asked.

"No. I'm happy here for now. When I'm not, I'll let myself go then."

"What do you mean by that, Jennifer?"

"Ghosts, remnants, spirits, whatever we're called, we're not trapped here, you know? When our bodies die and he takes our soul, we simply decide to stay until we're done. When that happens, we die again. I'm not done yet."

"But you were so distressed last time I met you."

"I was."

"Yet you're okay now."

"I am."

"I don't think I understand any of this," I groaned, slumping further into my seat.

"You have up days and down days, don't you?"

I nodded.

"So, why can't I have up days and down days?"

"But you're a ghost," I argued.

"And?" Jennifer asked, standing suddenly as if she'd had enough.

"Wait!" I called before she could disappear on me. "I just, I, erm . . . well, thank you. I don't know why you agreed to come and talk to me, but I'm so glad you did. Will I ever see you again?"

"That's up to you. After all, you've bumped into me twice now," she replied before disappearing out of the room.

"Twice?" I muttered to myself. Sitting there sipping my tea (which was by now stone cold), it finally came to me. It had been the night that Grammy had died. I'd raced through the hospital desperate to get to A&E, stopping abruptly when I saw Blake disappearing down a corridor. She'd bumped into me that night as well. *I'll be damned,* I thought to myself.

Chapter 17 – Blake

Saturday 20ᵗʰ April 2019

Emma had eventually gone back to her bed, but only after being chased out of the common room by 'Mr. Jovial.' Exhaustion had finally won its battle, and she'd fallen into a deep sleep, taking most of her bubble with her. Consequently, Blake was able to watch over her while she slept. A faint smile tugged at the corners of his mouth. Emma was adorable when she was at peace, although strange images flickered in his mind.

Blake had never needed to rest, he'd never felt the desire to lay his head down and sleep, and as a consequence, he was unable to comprehend what it was like for her when she did so. She looked to be content, but if that was the case, why were her dreams so disturbing? First of all, Joanne leapt into his peripheral vision, brandishing a flaming sword. She stood waving a blade that burped fire above her head, but before Blake could focus on her, she was gone, only to be replaced by a river on which Emma rafted. It meandered lazily along, passing through the quintessential British countryside. But the idyllic scene soon became one of torment when the water rose up in front of her forming an eighty-foot mass that undulated and writhed, dancing away to an unheard tune. Blake watched as Emma opened her mouth to scream, but before she could utter a sound, Cooper appeared and jumped into her arms. Where he'd come from, Blake had no idea! Dreams were a mystery to him, as were his feelings.

In the main, the complexity and depth of human emotion eluded him. While it was true that he'd lived an exceptionally long life and that he'd watched many thousands of people living theirs, without the ability to interact with any of them, he'd not had the opportunity to experience the full depth and breadth of sentiment. Of course, he'd thought he'd seen enough to fully understand people but in reality, he'd been ignorant. Because of his peculiar ability to witness each life at its end, he had millions of memories, but apparently they weren't enough; he'd suffered through the agony of labour but felt the overwhelming surge of love, he'd held the hand of a dying parent while feeling both relief and sorrow, and he'd enjoyed the tranquillity of a deserted beach on a warm, sunny day despite a racing heart and crippling anxiety. For many hundreds of years, he'd thought he'd understood. He'd been arrogant in his belief that mankind was no more complicated than the animals they chose to dominate. And then he'd met Emma.

After many centuries worth of monotony, she'd exploded into his life, giving him the opportunity to experience the world around him while also forcing him to re-evaluate everything he believed about those he was obliged to attend to. She was infuriatingly adamant about what she believed to be true, but sometimes her behaviour belied her words, and Blake knew (because of his ability to hear her thoughts) that she wasn't aware of this fact. She might be dichotomous, but it wasn't intentional. He'd heard her repeatedly reassure people that she was fine—and he knew without a doubt that she genuinely believed it—yet he'd watched her flinch at loud noises. Joanne's revelations had been interesting to say the very least. She'd demonstrated such compassion and understanding but had then gone on to attempt murder, claiming she was saving the world. It was perplexing!

What he really struggled with, what he was finding hard to grasp, was how the mere presence of Emma felt like a soothing balm against his own torrid emotions. For most of his life he'd been dissatisfied and irritated, he'd struggled with frustration, resentment, and envy. He'd lusted, but he'd never loved. In truth, he'd been jealous of everyone else because they could do whatever they wanted whenever they wanted, while his life had been constrained by the fact that he couldn't interact with the physical realm. He'd been forced into a life of servitude, having had no say in the role that was his to play. For nearly a thousand years, he'd had to reap people's souls, he'd had to observe history in the making, he'd had to watch from the sidelines while everyone else forged their own path. It had left him with a sour taste in his mouth until eventually his anger had burned into apathy. His ability to care had been reduced to ash, but somehow Emma had stoked the embers.

Blake knew without a doubt that he loved Emma, but why? Was it because she had half of his soul, or was there more to it? On their date, he'd assured her that it wasn't just because he was able to manifest with her by his side, and he believed that to be true because he'd wanted her before he knew what she could do for him, so why did he love? Why did anyone love those around them?

Standing there in the hospital, Blake finally concluded that he knew nothing about his own feelings. He'd longed for Emma from the moment he'd first laid eyes on her, but his desire was tempered by irritation. He'd been furious to learn that she could pull him to her. In fact, that ire continued to burble away in his veins, spiking whenever she inadvertently compelled him to do something. He'd come alive when they'd finally shared a kiss, feeling excited and nervous all at the same time. How was it possible for two opposing emotions to swirl around together in the same moment? And when she'd been attacked! Her fear had become his in an instant. He'd never before been immobilised in such a way, unsure how to act, held tight in the clutches of terror.

"Blake," Emma murmured in her sleep, her bubble suddenly swelling in size and capturing him in its net.

Blake, his musing disturbed, looked straight into the eyes of Mr. Jovial, whose mouth fell open in surprise. Blake didn't wait to hear what he was about to say, instead he translocated out of the way. He had no intention of being too far away from Emma any time soon, though, and so he reappeared almost instantaneously on the roof of the hospital immediately above where Emma slumbered. He knew everything that Jennifer had had to say and, while he wasn't convinced about her explanation, there clearly was something amiss.

Chapter 18 – Emma

Saturday 20ᵗʰ April 2019

"Dad! Where's Mum?" I exclaimed, catching sight of him as soon as he poked his head around the corner. Of course, it wasn't hard to miss him because he was huge. It wasn't uncommon for him to be described as a bear of a man, a teddy bear but a bear nonetheless.

I'd finally been released, and he was my lift home. His huge stride put him by my side in two swift steps, and I found myself pulled into one of his wraparound hugs before he answered my question. I slid my arms around his waist and nestled into the comfort that he offered. Sometimes my dad's love was a little on the suffocating side, but during the last eight weeks, I'd found myself welcoming his overbearing nature and leaning into him more and more frequently.

"She stayed home to prepare some lunch for you." My dad spoke without releasing me from his hold, unaware of the turn in my thoughts. At least some of the men in my life had the good grace to keep their noses out of my internal deliberations.

"Dad, you have to put me down eventually, you know?" I said after what felt like hours but was probably only mere moments.

"Hmmm," my dad's deep voice rumbled, resonating throughout my whole body. He squeezed tightly before stepping away from me. "What did the doctor say? I assume you're staying with us tonight."

"Erm, no. He gave me the all-clear." I might have been a little needy in the last eight weeks, but I hadn't been so needy that the thought of moving in with my parents had occurred, not even for one night.

"You shouldn't be alone after what happened though."

"I won't be alone. Blake will be with me."

"But—"

"Dad! I love you too, but I can't move back home with you and Mum."

"I didn't mean for it to be permanent, although . . ."

"No!"

"Okay, okay. I meant just for tonight anyway. It's Easter Sunday tomorrow after all." His face fell, and I could feel his disappointment coming off him in waves, not in the literal sense, not in the way that I could feel Blake's emotions, but his upset was fairly obvious by the slump of his shoulders.

"Cooper and Watson need me, Dad." I tried to let him down as gently as I possibly could. "They've already had one night alone. And I promise Blake will stay with me." I turned away from him to gather up my belongings, hoping to end the argument before it could really get started. Hurting my dad was not a favourite pastime of mine, but did he have to be sooo . . . well, so fatherly all the time.

"Where is Blake anyway? I thought he might have offered to collect you." There was an edge in my dad's voice that was new.

"He doesn't drive," I answered, ignoring the jibe. I was fairly certain that my dad liked Blake, other than the fact that I was his little girl and no one was ever going to be good enough for me, especially not someone who was a little on the quirky side.

"He doesn't drive?"

"No, he's never felt the need," I answered. "I'm ready," I added, standing up straight, my meagre belongings from the night before gathered together into the plastic bag that my mum had brought the pyjamas and slippers in. "Let's go."

While my dad and I made our way through the hospital on the way to his car, we chatted amiably about everything and nothing, but if I'm honest, I was distracted. I couldn't help but look at everyone I passed and wonder if they were ghosts. Jennifer had looked like a real, live, living person so how could I tell the dead apart? How many ghosts had I seen in my life without even realising it?

"What's up, pumpkin?" My dad asked suddenly after I'd not answered his last question quickly enough.

I sighed as quietly as I could before answering, "Nothing, honestly I'm fine."

My dad literally threw his head back and laughed, pausing to rest a hand on his midriff. Once upon a time, his stomach had been washboard flat, but age was starting to sneak up on him and there was no denying that he was getting bulkier around the middle. "Oh Emma, you can't pull the wool over my eyes, you know? I've always been able to tell when something was wrong with you."

"No, you haven't!" It was an automatic response for me to contradict him. In fact, I didn't even think about whether or not I believed what I'd said to be the truth.

"Haven't I?" My dad looked directly at me, his bushy eyebrows raised. He didn't wait for an answer before continuing. "You might have been able to trick your mum, but you've never been able to fool me."

"Daaad." I pulled a face and grabbed his hand to get him moving again. Never in my life had I had a serious one-on-one conversation with my dad about how I was feeling. And how would I even begin to explain some of what I was going through? Hey, Dad! My boyfriend's the one and only Grim Reaper. He's almost a thousand years old. My soul isn't really my own, it's part of his. Because of that, I can make him manifest. And on top of all of that, last night I had a fascinating conversation with this lovely young girl. Her name was Jennifer. Oh yes, and she was dead by the way.

"I might be able to help you know." My dad's usual baritone voice took on a bass-like quality, and I found myself wanting to confide in him, to tell him everything. But honestly, I didn't think he could handle it. If he even thought I was in danger of stubbing my toe, he'd give his life up for me. Imagine what he'd do if he knew what was really going on.

"Do you believe in ghosts?" I asked, suddenly curious to learn just how accepting my dad might be. My mum would never entertain the idea of a supernatural community; she was far too pragmatic for that, but my dad . . . who knew? He'd never hinted at any kind of belief system, he wasn't religious, he didn't go to church, he didn't even watch anything fantastical on the television, but then again maybe I'd never asked the right questions.

"That's . . . not what I was expecting," my dad said before falling silent. I was starting to think that he wasn't going to say anything else on the subject when eventually he opened his mouth again. What came out took me by surprise. "When you were a little girl, maybe two or three years old, you started chattering away to thin air when we were out and about. You'd say 'hello' and 'who are you?' and sometimes you'd point at nothing and say 'Daddy, look at him' yet there was never anyone there. Your mum and I dismissed it at first; we assumed you were just exercising your imagination as little kiddies often do. Your brother had been through a stage where everything was a dinosaur after all." My dad paused and smiled to himself, presumably at a memory of Scott. "I was worried though; I couldn't get the idea out of my head that what you were doing was somehow different. In the end I took you to the doctor; he said you'd probably created an imaginary friend to help you deal with some kind of trauma or loss. Well, you hadn't suffered a trauma, but Scott had just gone to school, and so I let myself believe that you were just missing your big brother. But do you know something, Emma? I never really believed that."

My mind was completely blown. I'd seen ghosts all along. I just couldn't remember seeing them. How was that even possible? A million and one questions buzzed inside my brain, each vying for attention, each desperate to be asked. But it was the obvious one that popped out. "What happened after that, Dad?"

"Your mum and I did as the doctor advised and treated you as though you had any number of imaginary friends. We even offered to let you invite one of them over for tea, but you always declined, saying that they couldn't leave where they were. Your brother started teasing you after that and eventually you just stopped talking to them. Occasionally I'd see you wave or smile at nothing though."

"When did I stop?"

"Who said you ever stopped?"

"I still do it?"

"You tell me."

Both of us fell silent then, each lost in our own thoughts. We'd made it back down the world's longest corridor and into the main entrance of the Vic before either of us spoke again.

"Dad?" The fact that I was asking a question was obvious by the tone of my voice. "Do you see that guy over there?" I pointed to where an older man was sitting on his own in the corner of the coffee shop that dominated the main entrance of the Vic. It was the same coffee shop where Ellie and I had had coffee and cake only a week previously. It had been quite busy then but now, at this time in the morning, it was reasonably quiet. Even if I hadn't gestured, there was very little chance that my dad could mistake who it was I meant.

"No, pumpkin, no, I don't."

"Dad?"

"Hmmm."

"Do you think I'm crazy?" I asked, even though I knew I wasn't. It was patently obvious to me that the older man was a ghost (what other explanation was there?), but if my dad couldn't even see him, what did he think was going on?

"No. I think you're different and special. I've always thought you were one of a kind."

"You're just saying that," I answered, bumping my hip into him affectionately.

"If you say so," my dad agreed.

"Why haven't you ever mentioned any of this before?"

"You never asked." It was a fairly simple answer but one that made me wonder if my dad meant more by it. However, before I had time to probe any further, I was forced to an abrupt stop, my path blocked by the older man from the coffee shop. He dipped his head and raised his fedora with a smile.

"Hello," I replied in response to his unspoken greeting. If my dad wondered who I was speaking to, he didn't comment, choosing instead to wait patiently.

"Jennifer and I talked this morning," the man said to me.

"You did? I assumed you avoided each other."

"Why would we do that?"

"You avoid *him*." I hoped my gentleman friend would know who I meant because I didn't want to mention Blake in front of my dad.

"That's different. He can make us move on, dissipate into the ether."

"Oh." There wasn't a lot else I could say to that.

"Jennifer explained what happened to you. She also told me her theory. She could be right, you know. But only a spirit empowered by a soul would be able to take control of the water in the way she described."

"Really?" I asked out loud while wondering how that was possible because Blake was adamant that all souls got reaped, the only exception being those that got cleaved.

"Really. The soul would also allow it to fight its compulsion."

"Its . . . never mind." I remembered what Jennifer had said about why she haunted the corridors of Blackpool Vic. "How do you know about all of this?"

"I've talked to other ghosts, older ones. Most of us wither and die over time but some of the really old ones have been here for centuries. They're older than he is. They remember a time when the Keeper of Souls would gift a soul to a spirit on occasion so that they could finish whatever it was they wanted to do."

"John could do that?"

"John could do almost anything. He was second only to God."

"Whoa!" My eyes widened into mini saucers.

"Anyway, my dear, I just thought I'd let you know. I'll leave you in the company of your father now." He winked and then disappeared before I had chance to say thank you, but when I looked over my shoulder, I saw that he was back in the coffee shop and waved goodbye.

"Well?" my dad asked before I had time to process what I'd learned.

I shrugged. "He just wanted to say hello, I think."

"Who was avoiding who?" Thankfully my dad had only heard my half of the conversation.

"I thought they all avoided each other but apparently not," I answered, too dazed to even think about withholding the truth.

"Who's him then?"

"Erm, you, dad. He avoided you so that you wouldn't walk through him."

"Poppycock," my dad answered, but he didn't push it any further.

Chapter 19 – Emma

Tuesday 23rd April 2019

Easter had been and gone by the time I was able to return to any of my weird and wonderful worry beads. I'd parked the one about Joanne, deciding simply to avoid her. Ellie was doing the same, although it was harder for her because she still had the inconvenience of living with her parents. But what about everything else? Was I being haunted? And if so, by who? And why? Also, who'd daubed blood on my front door? Because I didn't think that was connected. One of my ancestors had spoken about 'the darkness' and also about 'them.' It appeared as though two different 'baddies' were after me! Yippie!

Thankfully, because of the incident at Charlotte's, Easter had been relocated to my house even though I didn't really have the space. Regardless of the teeny, tiny size of my house, I didn't whinge when my mum suddenly announced that she'd be round at 9 a.m. sharp on Sunday morning and that I could help her with the prep work. In fact, I breathed a sigh of relief because at least my house had been designated a safe zone by my ancestors. I didn't fully understand what that meant, but I wasn't oblivious to the fact that I only ever felt that pesky breeze when I stepped over the threshold.

My mum and I had in fact spent a happy-ish morning preparing the turkey and chopping enough vegetables to feed an army before she'd declared that my house needed a quick clean. Doing chores wasn't exactly how I'd planned on spending Easter Sunday but, and I hated to admit it, by the time we were done, my little two-up, two-down had looked amazing! And she hadn't thrown too much of my stuff away. My mum hated clutter with a passion. She didn't have a sentimental bone in her body, and as a consequence, she didn't hold onto mementos. Personally I liked the odd knick-knack but the only ornaments that my mum deemed acceptable were photographs.

"You haven't put a picture of Blake up yet," she'd commented, halfway through the morning.

"No, I haven't got round to it," I'd replied as vaguely as possible.

"Perhaps we'll get a nice one of you both today."

"My arms are still bandaged," I'd argued, assuming that Blake would not want a camera thrust in his face and unsure if he would even show up in a photograph, what with him being a spectre that only I could see most of the time.

"Pfft, you can barely see your bandages with your sleeves down," she'd said, and that had been that. I'd known without a doubt that at some point during the day Blake and I would be forced to pose for our first couples shot. And I hadn't been wrong.

Despite the anxiety I'd felt at the prospect of having my picture taken, Easter had ended up being relatively pleasant. Blake had 'arrived' just before my dad and Scott and had been delighted to find that my mum had bought him his very own Easter egg. Then everyone had eaten far too much at the dinner table before somehow squeezing in a half tonne of chocolate each. All in all, it had been a good day, for me anyway. Cooper and Watson had probably thought that their sanctuary had been invaded.

The photograph had even turned out to be a nice one. I'd looked at it every day since Easter! "I still don't understand how it's possible for you to be caught on camera," I remarked, looking at it again before discarding my phone. I'd already viewed it eighty-nine million times, excited to have my first picture of Blake, and so the image was well and truly burned onto my retinas. I didn't really need to look at it anymore, all I had to do was close my eyes and I could see it clearly. It was a head and shoulders shot, so you couldn't see any of my squidgy bits or the fact that Blake had his arm around my waist, but you could see that our heads were leaning in the direction of each other. We looked very much in love, even though Blake was barely smiling. He wasn't scowling, though, so that was a win as far as I was concerned.

"You're the one who discovered it was possible."

"Did I?"

"Yes. After the accident in Las Vegas."

"Oh yes," I said aloud, wondering how I could possibly have forgotten such an important nugget of information.

The accident in Las Vegas had been something that I'd read about while idly spooling through Facebook. The driver of a bus had fallen asleep at the wheel, swerved across the highway, and collided with oncoming traffic. Eleven people had died, eight of them school children. And Blake had been there; he'd shown up in at least one of the images that had accompanied the news story.

"I wonder how many other pictures there are of you out there," I remarked absently, not really thinking about what I was insinuating.

"You think there are more?" Blake's words might have been structured as a statement, but his tone left no doubt in my mind that he was asking a question.

"It stands to reason: if there's one, why wouldn't there be more?"

"How are you going to find them?"

"Me? I wouldn't even know where to start." Why did Blake automatically assume he could dictate to those around him? Oh yes! Nearly a thousand years of believing he was hard done by. And I suppose he was, but oh my God! Sometimes I wondered how on earth I'd fallen for him, but the truth of it was that I'd been drawn to him like a moth to a flame. Or maybe like a piece of metal to a magnet. I was his, and he was mine. Maybe it was because we shared a soul and so had a connection no one else would ever understand. Maybe it was because of destiny or fate or whatever you wanted to call it. Maybe it was simply my doom. I didn't really know, and I couldn't really explain it. All I could say for definite was that when I was in his arms, I felt whole, the continual buzz of noise ebbed away until all I could hear was the beauty of silence.

"Use your phone."

"And search for what exactly?"

"The Keeper of Souls."

"That won't work. No one has ever heard of the Keeper of Souls. If they were going to tag you at all, they'd use the words 'grim' and 'reaper.'"

"But I am the Keeper of Souls." I felt Blake's fury writhe in my own gut.

I rolled my eyes. We'd had this argument before. "I'm aware, but no one else even knows you exist, and anyone that does believe in you would call you the Grim Reaper."

Blake all but huffed his displeasure. "What would you suggest then?" he asked, taking on a sarcastic tone that I was all too familiar with because it was one that I used on a regular basis.

"Erm . . ." Nothing immediately sprang to mind. "Why don't weee . . ." I started talking in the vain hope that an idea would form, but when the lightbulb failed to provide illumination, I asked a question, "What was the last catastrophe you attended?"

"The one in Cologne."

"Right, let's look that up and see what we can see." As plans went, it wasn't the most in-depth one I'd ever hatched, but I retrieved my phone from where I'd dumped it earlier, opened up a news app, hit the search icon, and typed in the word 'Cologne.' A number of options appeared in red text, I selected one and was redirected to a page of articles. At the very top of the page, there was a picture of the Cathedral, underneath which a caption read 'Carnage in Cologne.' One more click and I was into the detail of the article and spooling through the text.

"Ding, ding, ding, we have a winner," I muttered when my eyes caught sight of Blake in one of the many accompanying images.

"Let me see," Blake demanded.

I selected the picture to make it full size and turned my phone so that we could both look at it. It was a wide screenshot of the Domplatte, bathed in the blue lights of the polizei. People were scattered everywhere, and there was a section of ground that had been covered over with a tarpaulin. I shuddered at the thought of what was hidden from view. Blake stood off to one side, dressed as usual in his preferred black with a look of nonchalance on his face.

"What on earth happened?" I asked. Among everything else that had occurred in the last few days, Blake had barely mentioned the shooting.

"Heidi fired at random before taking her own life."

"But why? Why would anyone do that?"

"She was unwell," Blake replied. His answer told me nothing really, but a wisp of sorrow blew through me.

"What is it?"

"When I reaped her soul, I watched her life unfold before my eyes. She was diagnosed with schizophrenia and told that the voices and the visions were nothing more than hallucinations, but what if they weren't? What if they were demons?"

"I suppose it's possible." I hated to admit it, but after what I'd learned recently, what else could I say? "If there are demons, though, how come you've never seen one? You see gho—" Blake glared at me. ". . . I mean remnants, don't you?"

"Yes."

"So, how come you've never seen a demon? Or maybe you have and you didn't realise it," I paused, wondering if that were possible, knowing that Blake would never admit it even if it was. "What did Abaddon say again?" I asked. Blake had filled me in on his meeting with her, but I couldn't remember the details.

"Only that I wouldn't find one. Clearly they have a way of hiding what they are, or else they avoid me," he finished. His hurt stung in the same way a paper cut would. It wasn't so painful that I felt like I was going to die, but it still smarted. It was time to move the conversation on.

"How do you distinguish between the living and the dead? Jennifer looked real to me."

"She is real. She's just not alive."

"You know what I mean." I sighed in exasperation. No matter how much he grew, I didn't think Blake the pedant was ever going to leave us. "So, how do you tell them apart?"

"Remnants are duller."

"Jennifer didn't look grey."

"I didn't say grey, I said duller."

"Huh, maybe you can see the absence of a soul then?"

"I don't believe that's it. I'd never seen a soul until I saw you being attacked."

"Hmmm. What does Seith make of all this anyway?"

"Seith doesn't offer opinions."

"Did Seith not even have any ideas as to who could be haunting me?"

"No one is haunting you."

Anger engulfed me in an instant, forcing me to act without thinking. "If no one is haunting me, then what the hell is happening?" I stood, grabbed Blake's hand, and pulled him to his feet. We were out in the back garden before he had time to object. From inside, it had looked incredibly inviting. The sun shone brightly, bathing my own little slice of the great British countryside in a soft yellow light that turned the grass an emerald green colour. However, I'd barely set foot outside when a breeze blew. It started out gentle, lifting the hairs on my arms and causing goosebumps to erupt, but within seconds, I was being battered by gales that were so strong I could barely set one foot in front of the other. Forcing myself to move, I reached for the outside tap and turned it on. Water flowed freely, but before it had even splashed onto the ground, it veered in my direction.

"Try telling me that that's natural," I all but shouted as the wind tore the words from my mouth.

The effort it took to say anything at all left me exhausted, and even though the door was only a couple of feet away, I could barely turn, let alone make my way back into the safety of my home. Before I knew what was happening, Seith had appeared, and I found myself nosed back into the house and into Blake's waiting arms. Seith followed, forcing Blake and me to take a step backwards, before laying himself (herself?) on the floor. Quite casually, he laid his muzzle on his front paws, effectively blocking the route to the back door. Seith was male, right? Blake had never said one way or the other, and I couldn't exactly ask.

"I left the tap on," I said. My words were muffled because Blake held me tightly within the circle of his arms. Seith must have heard, though, because he lifted his head and bared his teeth. I sensed that a growl sounded inside Blake's mind based on the ripple of emotion that washed over me and the welter of images that flashed briefly in my mind. Despite the circumstances, I felt a momentary spike of pleasure at being able to read Blake's mind. "I guess I'll just text Ellie then," I muttered, which must have been the right answer because Seith settled back down in the doorway. Apparently I was now a prisoner in my own home, at least until we'd figured out what was going on and how to deal with it.

Chapter 20 – Ellie

Tuesday 23rd April 2019

Ellie's phone vibrated in her pocket, alerting her to the fact that she'd just received a text. Scott's face swam up to the surface of her mind, and a slight thrill ran through her body. Ever since they'd held hands in the hospital, he'd been texting her more frequently. His messages never really said anything more than 'hey you,' but Ellie was hopeful that they meant something more. And even if they didn't, his interest was a welcome distraction from everything else that was going on.

Emma had called it; Ellie had been in love with Scott for as long as she could remember, but she'd never allowed herself to think about it. She'd never even admitted it to herself, preferring instead to hide her emotions behind a wall of innuendo and laughter. She'd certainly never voiced her feelings, which made it a miracle that Emma had picked up on them really.

What was she going to do about Emma and her mum? She felt like her heart was being torn in two. There was nothing she wouldn't do for Emma. Grammy had made sure of that. There was no way she'd ever allow anyone to hurt her, but she had no choice other than to forgive her mum, who'd been brought up to believe that if the Key ever met Blake, there was only one course of action. And really, what did one life matter when compared with the fate of the world?

Dipping her hand inside of her tunic pocket, Ellie retrieved her phone. Disappointment swallowed her whole before the guilt hit. The text was from Emma, not Scott. The more Ellie thought about it, the more confident she became that Grammy had had a hand in how close she and Emma had become. She'd been the one to enrol her mum in the same school as Sandra after all. She'd encouraged their friendship through the years. Of course, Grammy had been in on the secret, so she must have done everything for a reason. Grandpa Harold had broken the rules when he'd told her all about the Keeper of Souls and his purpose as the Guardian. Only the heir was ever meant to know, but Grandpa Harold had never kept anything from Grammy. The only thing that Ellie hadn't worked out was why Grammy had picked her mum to carry Grandpa Harold's legacy after him, and not one of her sons. She was certain that Grammy had been in on the decision.

So, I did a thing and now I could do with some help. Blake and I had a tiff. Somehow I ended up outside. I turned the tap on to prove I was being haunted. You should have seen what happened! Don't worry, I'm okay. Seith nosed me back into the house but now he won't let me back out again. Please help! Can you come and turn the tap off? Xx

Was it possible to laugh, cry, and shake your head in disbelief all at the same time? Emma's snarky behaviour was going to be the death of her one day. She never learned! It was just like her to throw herself in harm's way to prove a point. Maybe she, Ellie, wouldn't have to face a horde of demons after all because at this rate, Emma would solve humanity's latest crisis all on her own—suicide by ghost. Now that had a ring to it!

Not that I mind coming over, but can't Blake do it? Xx
Seith won't let either of us outside. Xx

"Andrew?" Ellie shouted, glancing at her watch. There were only ten minutes of her shift left; she was fairly certain Andrew would let her go early.

"Yes," he replied from somewhere nearby. Ellie was in the corridor that ran the length of Cedar's Veterinary Centre, but she had no idea where Andrew was. She looked around her before arbitrarily pulling open the door closest to her, the one into the room where the overnighters were kept.

Bingo! Whenever Andrew was lost, he was usually found where the animals were. "Hi." She beamed at him. Andrew was such a sweetheart that it was impossible not to love him. He was gruff by nature, curt with people, blunt and outspoken, but oh, how he loved animals! He poured his heart and soul into caring for them. "Do you mind if I scoot? Emma needs a hand with something."

"Go. And tell her not to even think about coming back until she's fully healed." Her start date had been pushed back again.

"Tell her yourself! You know she's itching to come back to work. She's gutted not to be here today."

Andrew harrumphed. "It was one thing when she'd been attacked, but now she's been in an explosion as well. She needs time."

"She loves this place though. And she's worried about letting you down."

"Pfft. Her job will be here waiting for her."

"I know that. I'll tell her. Thanks so much."

"Ellie," Andrew called as she turned to leave. "Emma will be okay, you know."

Ellie paused before answering, "I know. Thanks, Andrew."

"You need to stop worrying about everything. You'll be grey by the time you're forty if you're not careful."

"I'll try," Ellie offered as much reassurance as she could. If only he knew the half of it! She left the room before Andrew could say anything else, and it wasn't long until she was opening the door of Emma's house. "Hi!" she shouted, doing her utmost to sound cheery. She spotted both Emma and Blake immediately, sitting together on the sofa underneath the front room window, but what captured her attention was the sight of Seith. Emma had always described him as an oversized German shepherd, and while her description was accurate, it also wasn't quite right. Seith was massive, with upright pointed ears, a long cone-shaped muzzle, and amber-coloured eyes that sparkled with intellect. No German shepherd had ever looked at her with such human understanding.

Ellie didn't dare move a muscle while Seith rose and stalked in her direction. She was trapped by the intensity of his very presence, never mind the sheer bulk of him. For several long seconds, Ellie stared open mouthed at Seith and Seith stared right back at her. There was no hostility in his gaze, but there was something. He appraised Ellie in a way that shouldn't have been possible. It was almost as though he could see something in her, like he was weighing up her moral compass maybe.

Time slowed down, and all Ellie could do was hold her breath. Frozen as she was, she allowed her thoughts to drift until Seith huffed in her face, apparently giving her the seal of approval. "I'll just turn the outside tap off, shall I?" she announced, strolling towards the back door as though she had not a care in the world, which was all an act, of course!

Ellie stepped out of the house and breathed in the fresh air, filling her lungs with cool, calming oxygen. A smile danced on the corner of her lips; Emma's garden was drenched in the sunlight of early spring, the hedgerow was growing greener by the day, and plant life was slowly awakening. Life was good, apart from the fact that her best friend might inadvertently bring about the end of the world and she was apparently meant to stop it by killing her. Oh, and the fact that her mum had already tried to do just that. She shook her head at the absurdity of the situation, turned the tap off, and returned to the house, carefully stepping over Seith's tail. He seemed to have decided it was his job to guard the back of the house.

"All done," Ellie announced. "Brew?" She looked over her shoulder and saw both Emma and Blake nodding, albeit Blake was nodding much more enthusiastically than Emma. Blake loved to be included in anything and everything involving food and drink.

While she waited for the kettle to boil, Ellie snuck odd glances at Seith, hoping that she saw something with the gift of sight that Abaddon had given her. He was the enigma in all of this after all. Ellie knew what part she had to play, even if she didn't like it and had no intention of going through with it. She understood Emma's role and who Blake was, but Seith . . . what was his purpose? He'd rolled onto his side while she'd been pottering about in the kitchen and most certainly seemed to be nothing more that a dog who was sound asleep. Every now and again his back paw twitched, so perhaps he was dreaming, perhaps he was just a dog chasing rabbits in the land of nod. Ellie didn't think so, but no matter how hard she stared she couldn't *see* anything. She'd never really tried to use her new sight, though, so maybe she was doing it wrong. Or maybe Seith was just a dog.

"So, what are we going to do about the fact that Emma is clearly being haunted then?" Ellie asked as she handed mismatched mugs of tea to Emma and Blake before returning to the kitchen to retrieve her own drink and a packet of biscuits. Emma was going through a hobnob phase, and so that's all Ellie had been able to find in the cupboard.

"Emma is not being haunted," Blake declared.

"It's the only explanation, Blake," Emma waded into the debate, her voice throbbing with just as much passion as Blake's. Both were stubborn. Perhaps sharing a soul made them similar?

"It's not possible. You know that a remnant would have to be powered by a soul if they were going to attack you with the elements."

"And?"

"And what?"

"A ghost must have got hold of a soul then."

"That's not possible."

"Isn't it?"

"You're implying that I've not done my job properly."

"I'm not implying anything, Blake. I'm saying it outright, you messed up and missed a soul somewhere along the way. The only other explanation is that John gave one away, but if that was the case, why would that ghost wait until now to attack?"

Ellie had a sneaky suspicion that Emma was using the word 'ghost' on purpose, but before she could say anything to diffuse the situation, Seith rolled onto his stomach, lifted his head, and barked. No sound came from his mouth, but a strange sensation reverberated through Ellie's entire body. It was as though a silent bomb had been dropped nearby, or else a sonic boom had been triggered in the next room. She felt as though she'd been punched in the gut, her stomach muscles clenched tightly together as a wave of adrenaline washed over her. The tea shook in her hand, and upstairs something smashed to the floor. In her eyeline, Emma flinched, and much to Ellie's surprise, Blake paled.

Blake had been isolated for so long that he had yet to develop a poker face. His emotions flickered and danced across his face. Ellie was able to read each in turn, and as a consequence, she witnessed the exact moment when Blake accepted that he may have had a part to play in what was happening to Emma. Annoyance built into anger but was quickly replaced with doubt. Doubt rapidly transformed into guilt, which then almost immediately became anguish and fear.

"Seith agrees you are being haunted," he eventually muttered, and all credit to Emma, she bit back a sarcastic reply, opting to pull Blake into her instead, wrapping him up in a comforting hug.

Chapter 21 – Emma

Tuesday 23rd April 2019

Time stood still for a second while Blake processed whatever it was that Seith had barked at him. Because I was at the almost-but-not-quite-able-to-read-Blake's-mind stage, I was submerged in a torrent of conflicting emotions while he worked through what he was feeling. My blood started to boil with irritation but then anxiety built and my stomach dropped ten thousand feet for no discernible reason before a weight like no other settled on my shoulders. Lastly paralysis crept over my limbs, freezing me where I sat.

When Blake eventually spoke, I expected an argument, but instead all I got was muted acceptance. Poor Blake! I nestled into the side of him, sliding my arms around his stomach, while a new emotion took hold, one that was very much my own. Put simply, I loved Blake with all my heart.

"So," Ellie said, now sitting on the second sofa in the lounge, the one opposite the television. "What do we do now?" she asked, smiling sweetly before sipping her tea.

"Erm . . . I have no idea. How on God's Earth do we find out who the hell is haunting me? And even if we do find out, what can we actually do about it?"

"Well, I think I know how we can work out who it is, assuming the soul isn't one that John handed out. And surely Blake can just . . . you know . . ." Ellie's words trailed off into nothing as she mimicked swinging a scythe with her spare hand. Or at least that's what I assumed she was doing. For all I knew, she could have been swatting at an imaginary fly or casting a spell with a pretend wand.

"My weapon is not a toy." Evidently Blake thought that Ellie had been miming death by blade too.

"I never said it was, did I?" Ellie replied, a smile on her face. From me, that statement would have sounded sarcastic, but somehow Ellie made it sound perfectly innocuous. "It would work, though, wouldn't it?"

"I suppose so," Blake conceded. Biscuit crumbs fell from his mouth, reminding me that I needed to have a discussion with him about etiquette. "I heard that," he added.

"Heard what?" Ellie asked while I turned beetroot red. Oh, how I desperately wanted to be able to turn the tables on him and read his mind all of the time.

"Never mind," I muttered. "So, how do we find this creep? I've had enough of being held captive."

"We do an internet search."

"Erm, Ellie, honey, I don't know what you've been drinking lately, but we can't simply do a search for 'what dastardly fiend has decided to make Emma's life a misery this week?'"

"Well, d'oh! Of course not! But I'm assuming this person isn't exactly one of the good guys, and Blake," Ellie physically shifted in her seat, all of her attention focussed on the love of my life, "you said that dark souls were rare, so to find the ghost . . ."

"Remnant," Blake interjected.

". . . all we need to do is search for who died when Blake last, you know . . . ." This time, instead of swiping at thin air, Ellie mimed slicing her own throat with her perfectly manicured nails. Her nails were trimmed short (policy for staff at Cedar's Veterinary Centre) and painted a bright neon yellow colour, which made me suspicious. Ellie only ever painted her nails when she was going out or was aiming to impress.

Note to self, I thought, *follow up on the nails.*

"I don't—" Blake started to object, but I cut him off, dismissing Ellie's idea.

"We can't do that."

"Why not?"

"It won't work. We'd need to know at least something about the person who died."

"We already know enough," Ellie declared firmly, her column of steel asserting itself. When Ellie had decided on something, there was no changing her mind. "We know it's a grade-A asshole, and Blake can tell us the person's life story because of his soul reading thing. He can also tell us where he was when he did the slicing and what date it was, can't you?" Ellie dazzled Blake with one of her sunbeam smiles, and I knew I'd lost the fight already. "Once we know a little more about whoever is doing the haunting, then we can set a trap." Her eyes literally sparked with delight.

"Fine," I mumbled, slumping back in my seat and slurping my tea like a bored teenager who'd just been told that, like it or not, they were going to have to play nice with the next-door neighbour's kids.

"The last soul I used the weapon on was Peter Collins."

"Well, I'm assuming it's not him because we all know you sliced his soul in two. So, who was the one before him?"

Blake huffed and then frowned. I concentrated on what he might be thinking or feeling and caught a glimpse of a cobbled alleyway at night. It was dark because there was no real light source other than from where the alleyway intersected with the main road. There wasn't even a moon; odd stars did their best to shine brightly but most of the sky was hidden behind thick clouds that drifted lazily from left to right. The ground was wet underfoot, but it didn't appear to be raining. Hidden in the shadows was a wraith-like figure dressed in inky-blue jeans, a dark roll-neck jumper, and a black leather jacket, zipped up the middle. Her features were pulled as taut as a violin string because her hair had been pinned tightly back into a high ponytail with a plain elastic band. She was all about sharp angles and straight lines. While I was still absorbing the details that brought the woman to life, a pained expression flicked across her face and her eyes clouded with doubt and fear. She lifted her left hand in the direction of her head but before she could react further, the life drained from her and she slowly toppled to the floor. Her corpse hadn't even stopped moving when a shade rose up from her body. And then Blake's blade swung into view.

I gasped in shock and jerked upright in my seat. What had been an idle can-I-even . . . should-I-try . . . oh-go-on-then thought had suddenly become very real. The lounge had dissolved around me, and I'd been pulled into Blake's memory. My heart was thumping so hard in my chest that I feared my ribs would be cracked open and torn apart. The blood surged in my ears, and I heard the roaring sound of the ocean despite being some miles inland. And then the image blurred and changed. As it crystallised and refocussed, I saw myself sitting with Ellie on a comfortable-looking sofa just inside the doorway of a coffee shop. Understanding didn't come straight away, but I did notice the warmth spreading slowly across the whole of my lap. Panicked, I looked down to see that there was now a pool of tea quickly soaking into my jeans.

"Urgh," I muttered just as it dawned on me what I had seen. "Oh no!" I whispered, my voice harsh, filled with sorrow and dismay.

"What?" Ellie asked. "Who is it?"

"It's me," I answered. Ellie looked baffled, forcing me to explain. "As Blake swung his scythe to cleave the last dark soul he came across, I pulled him to me. Blake missed. I'm the reason I'm being haunted."

"It was Saturday the 9th of February this year," Blake supplied.

"We were at the Trafford Centre, and I idly thought about Blake."

"But I thought all souls were reaped regardless of what else you were doing?" Ellie asked.

"They always have been," Blake muttered. "But only I can use the weapon, and I've never been interrupted before." Anger had clearly marched into Blake's psyche and taken root. His body, which had been turned towards me, was now rigidly taut and he was leaning ever so slightly away from me. His back was straight, and his shoulders were square.

I'm sorry, I whispered in the silence of my mind.

You blamed me, he answered curtly.

I didn't blame you, not exactly, I bit back. Apologising was not exactly one of my fortes. Besides which, while I was sorry, it wasn't like it was my fault. Not exactly anyway. I hadn't known who Blake was then. And I certainly hadn't had any idea that I could pull him to me with nothing more than a stray thought.

"Can't the copies use your scythe?" Ellie asked, interrupting my silent argument with Blake. I was absolutely positively certain that she'd picked up on his changing emotions because A) she was quite astute, and B) and it didn't take a psychic connection to read his body language. Thunderclouds looked more welcoming than he did, in fact they would have quaked in fear and fled the room if they'd come face-to-face with him. But she didn't let on, continuing to play happy families as though there was nothing more normal than drinking tea, eating biscuits, and discussing how to stop a pesky little haunting.

"No."

"Why not?"

"I don't know. Whenever a dark soul has needed to be dealt with, I've felt compelled to take the required action."

"Huh," Ellie replied, a faint frown ghosting her oval-shaped face. She was clearly working her way through everything that she'd learned . . . that we'd both learned actually. Blake didn't often discuss his work, so it was news to me that he always did cleavings himself. "So, it's possible then, isn't it?" Ellie continued. "If you didn't finish the job . . ."

"Because of Emma," Blake interjected through gritted teeth.

"Well, yes, because of Emma." Ellie smiled at me apologetically. "But for whatever reason, it's possible that there's a dark soul out there running amok. And if it's possible, it stands to reason that that's our ghost?"

"Remnant," Blake corrected while I launched into one-hundred-and-one questions.

"Does it?" I asked. "Are we assuming that whoever is haunting me is using their own soul as the power source? How can we be certain that that woman—"

"What woman?" Ellie asked.

"The last dark soul, the one that Blake, erm, well, you know . . . ." I'd been going to say 'missed,' but I didn't think that would go down well given Blake's current mood. "Anyway, it was a woman."

"Interesting. Women are more vindictive than men. In many ways, this makes much more sense if it's a woman who's haunting you."

"Why?"

"Well, she's probably pissed at Blake for killing her . . ."

"I didn't kill her."

"Yadda, yadda. I know that, but she probably doesn't. So, she's pissed and she can't take it out on you because you're, well you know, you. So, she's taking it out on Emma. Revenge is a dish best served cold and all that."

"Okay, but what if her soul is being used by another remnant?" I'd decided to use the correct terminology in an attempt to appease Blake, although his emotions were already cooling down again. The seed that Ellie had planted (that someone was using me to get to him) was growing nicely inside of him, and he was starting to feel queasy.

"That's a good question. Is that even possible, Blake?"

"What?" Blake asked curtly, clearly still in a bit of a funk.

"The old man at the Vic implied it was," I answered, even though Ellie had directed her question at Blake. "Bollocks!" I muttered.

"I think we'll just have to assume that that's not what happened here or else we'll never move forwards. So, let's assume it's her." Ellie was clearly excited. "What did you see when she died?"

Blake paused, presumably taking stock of what he'd learned, but I decided against intruding on his thoughts after last time. "It's the act of reaping or cleaving a soul that lets me see the life that has been lost."

"Meaning?"

"Meaning that he doesn't know anything about her," I answered confidently, able to deduce what Blake had left unsaid even though I hadn't snooped on his internal dialogue.

"Damn and blast!" Ellie cursed.

"But you may still be able to find her because I do know where I was."

My stomach lurched as a ripple of fear, tinged with a smidge of excitement, spread outwards from my core. Finally! It was all going to be over.

"Well then, where were you?" Ellie was clearly as eager as I was to have this over and done with.

After Blake told her, Ellie hit the internet while I sat in a daze. Was this it? Was it finally over? Or was there some other big-bad waiting in the wings to make my life a misery when the ghost had been dispatched? My nan had implied there were two different threats looming. I racked my brains, trying to remember exactly what she'd said, something about . . . the darkness . . . something about that needing to be what I focussed on for now. 'For now' sounded a little on the ominous side, but I'd been so wrapped up in the fact that I was obviously being haunted, I hadn't really worried about anything else. And of course, there was the whole thing about my boyfriend being a portal into hell. I hadn't really faced up to the fact that angels and demons walked the earth yet, were technically trapped here on Earth because Blake, unlike his predecessor, wasn't able to banish them.

"I've found something," Ellie announced, breaking into the silence that had fallen. Even Seith lifted his head and looked quizzically at Ellie. It was remarkable how much he could say without ever speaking a single word.

"Really? That was quick."

"Well, it might not be anything; I don't want you getting your hopes up just yet. But I think this is the person." Ellie turned her phone so that Blake and I could see. Seith thumped his paw on the floor, unhappy at being excluded. Ellie quickly turned her phone again, but I'd seen enough—it was definitely the person I'd seen when I'd snooped on Blake's memory.

"It's her, isn't it?" I said, looking at Blake for confirmation.

"Yes, assuming she's the one doing this."

"Well, the timing works, right? And all of the little snippets of information we've gathered fit together." I could feel myself getting more excited as I worked through what we knew. "We know that spirits can control the elements from what Jennifer told me. We know that only those with a soul are powerful enough to do any damage. I believe you've reaped every other soul in your lifetime, and if we all agree that it's one and the same in terms of the person doing this . . . ." I trailed off into silence, unsure how to articulate what I was thinking anymore. The idea that in life a person was made up of a body, a spirit, and a soul wasn't the easiest thing to understand, especially when each of those three things could be viewed of as independent entities. While I assumed that the spirit of one person could use the soul of another, could a spirit also use someone else's body? That idea was kind of creepy, that would mean zombies were a thing. I might have accepted ghosts as being real, but there were limits to what I was okay with.

"Yes, the timing works," Blake concurred.

"So, who is she?" I asked.

Ellie read from her phone, "An unidentified body was found—"

"Unidentified?" I interrupted. "But that means we still don't know who she is."

"Hold your horses!" Ellie looked up from her phone, grinning at me, her eyes bright. "An unidentified body was found in an alleyway in the heart of the city last night. The body is thought to be that of Anais Bechard, believed to be the most notorious paid assassin of modern times, although proof of her crimes has thus far eluded the police. Confirming that the body is indeed that of Ms. Bechard will be almost impossible because little is known about this prolific killer. Sources advise however that the body is almost certainly hers because in her pocket, there were a small number of bone fragments, all dyed blood red. Anais always left a coloured sliver of bone in the left cheek of each and every one of her victims. It was her calling card."

"That's just weird. Why would a murderer leave a piece of bone in the mouth of everyone she kills?"

"Really? That's what you want to focus on?"

"Well, yeah. It's odd."

"Never mind the fact that we're talking about a gun for hire. Someone who kills indiscriminately as long as the price is right. Someone who'll double-tap their own granny."

"Double-tap?" I exclaimed. "Who are you, and what have you done with my best friend. She doesn't use words like 'double-tap.'"

Ellie sniffed disdainfully before continuing, "No one really knows who Anais Bechard is. It's entirely possible that the name is . . . oh, this isn't good for us."

"What, what does it say?"

"Anais Bechard might not be her real name."

"Crap!" I cursed.

"It doesn't matter," Blake interjected.

"What do you mean, it doesn't matter?"

"All names have power, even if they are given rather than real."

"Huh," Ellie and I answered in unison, if 'huh' could be considered as an answer.

"What else does it say about Little Miss Murderer then?" I asked.

Ellie read the rest of the article quickly before summarising. "Anais Bechard is believed to be responsible for more than fifty kills. She was a ghost, and I don't mean that in the literal sense. Apparently within a certain sector of society, it was well known that if you wanted to off someone, you contacted Anais. No one ever found any evidence at the kill sites, and there's never been a way to link her with any of the crimes. She could literally be anyone. There's even a rumour that she might in fact be a he, but no one knows for sure. The police have been hunting her for years, but they've got absolutely nothing to go on."

"Wow, that's crazy."

"Isn't it though? If it hadn't been for the baggie of bones, the body in the alley would have been recorded as a Jane Doe."

"How did she die?"

"Bad luck by the look of it; she had a brain haemorrhage. Apparently, it would have been almost instantaneous."

"That's what we saw, isn't it, Blake?"

Blake nodded. "Yes, it did look like a brain haemorrhage."

"Fantastic! So, now what?"

"Now, we end this. I will not have your life put in danger again," Blake replied.

"Can we be a little more specific than that? How exactly are we going to end it?" I asked, worry coursing through my veins. I wasn't only frightened for myself though; I was afraid for Blake's safety too. When he was next to me, he was corporeal, and presumably that meant he could be hurt.

"Don't worry about me," Blake responded to my unspoken fears.

"Of course I worry about you, it's part and parcel of the whole deal."

A faint smile crossed Blake's face, causing it to soften. Blake was devastatingly handsome anyway but throw in an upturned mouth and my insides melted. "I'm going to call Miss Anais Bechard to me. I am then going to do what I was supposed to do all those weeks ago and slice her soul in two, releasing its negative energy into the ether so that it will dissipate and disperse. And then I am going to find a way to exorcise her."

"Wait! Wait! I know a way to do that," Ellie piped up.

"You do?"

"Yes, you told me."

"I did?" Ellie and I talked and texted every day, but nothing I'd said to her in the last few days sprung to mind.

"Yep, you said that Jennifer told you she avoided Blake because he could compel her to leave. So surely, all you have to do, Blake, is give the order."

"Well, we'll soon find out, won't we?"

Chapter 22 – Blake

Tuesday 23rd April 2019

Blake stepped out from the sanctity of Emma's house and into her garden, his stomach churning. He'd never experienced anxiety before, so the unsettled feeling that gripped him was new. He finally understood what people meant when they said they were paralysed by fear. His heart was racing and his feet felt leaden, but somehow he forced himself to move forwards, half hoping that each step would take him outside of Emma's bubble. Once upon a time he'd wanted to experience everything that life had to offer but now he found himself revising his ambitions.

Blake had never before set out with the sole purpose of doing anything. Even when he'd rescued Emma from her attacker, he hadn't planned it—he'd just acted on instinct. How did one go about planning something such as what he needed to do? He wasn't worried for himself; nothing could harm him. He'd walked freely across Flanders Fields while the battle raged because he could, because neither bullets nor grenades could cause him any harm. But what if he failed? What would that mean for Emma?

Emma's garden was soaking up the last few rays of the late afternoon sun. It was too bright for what he had planned, too colourful. Her borders, filled with clematis, herbs, hebes, lavender, buddleia, and bluebells, were slowly coming back to life, reawakened by the turning of the seasons and the return of spring. Little splashes of colour could be found among the hardy plants, thanks to the bluebells that were already flowering. The deep violet-blue of the downward-facing, bell-shaped flowers provided bright highlights against the emerald green of the surrounding foliage. At the bottom of the garden, the hedgerows were transforming once again, changing from a tangle of spiked thorns and woodish bramble into a luscious border that would soon bear fruit.

Blake had always believed that all he was able to do was reap the souls of the dying, cleaving those that had turned black. He'd never been responsible for anyone's death, hampered as he was by his inability to interact with the world around him. And even though he knew remnants existed, he'd never dealt with one of them before. As he'd explained to Emma on more than one occasion, they avoided him for reasons of their own. If Jennifer were to be believed, it was because he could 'send them away.' Ellie was confident that that meant he could deal with Anais, but Blake himself wasn't so sure. He'd always been certain about the extent of his capabilities. Surely he would have known if he had the ability to control the dead. Still, at the very least he could do what he should have done when he'd first met Anais; at the very least he could remove her soul. While that wouldn't entirely deal with the problem, it would make Anais less of a threat.

When Blake reached the end of the patio, he turned and glanced back at the house. Seith was now sat on his haunches outside while Emma and Ellie were standing just inside the glass doors, watching him. Blake had extracted promises from them both that they would remain inside the house no matter what happened and no matter what they saw. He had absolutely no intention of letting Anais harm a single hair on Emma's head, and while he was more ambivalent about Ellie's fate, he recognised that Emma would be distraught if anything happened to her best friend.

The pair were extreme opposites. Not only did Emma stand four inches taller than Ellie, she was rounded where Ellie was slight. But more than that, where Emma was the embodiment of summer with her copper-coloured hair and sun-kissed skin, Ellie, with her much paler skin and icy blue eyes, was winter brought to life. Both smiled encouragingly at him. He turned back to the garden.

"Anais Bechard." Blake spoke the words quietly, holding the image of Anais firmly in his mind. He'd only seen her on the day of her death, but his recall was excellent. He pictured her dressed as she'd been that day, in dark jeans, a dark jumper, and a black jacket, with her hair pulled tightly into a ponytail on the top of her head. She had a triangular-shaped face with high cheekbones and a pointed chin. Her eyes were narrow, and her lips were thin. In another life she'd have made a striking catwalk model.

"Anais Bechard," Blake said again, confident that Anais could hear him. "An-ais Be-chard," he said for a third time, pronouncing the words exactly.

"Mais oui," Anais replied lightly, finally appearing in front of Blake, a serpentine smile on her face. "You called?" she drawled, changing her accent from French to Texan, while buffing her nails lightly on the front of her jacket.

Blake clearly heard Emma and Ellie gasp behind him. Emma, he knew, had always been able to see remnants, but to his knowledge, Ellie had not. Either the fact that both he and Anais were still in Emma's bubble was allowing her to see Anais, or perhaps Abaddon's gift of sight was at play.

"Why are you doing this?" he asked. He'd had no intention of holding a conversation with Anais, but the words slipped out without his control.

Did you do that? he asked Emma, his eyes still focussed on his foe.

I was thinking it; I didn't expect you to ask it though, Emma replied.

"Because I want to," Anais answered before Blake could question Emma further. "You ended my life, and so I will take hers." She waved a hand in the direction of Emma. "They may have warded the house, but she can't stay in there forever, can she?"

"They? Who's 'they'?" Emma shouted from where she stood.

"Mon cherie," Anais purred, taking a step in Emma's direction. "Don't you know? You're quite important in some circles, what with being the Key and all that. Of course," she sniffed, "I don't care about any of that. I just want what I'm owed."

"He didn't take your life, you know. He isn't responsible for anyone's death. You had a brain haemorrhage; it was a quirk of fate." Emma remained safely within the boundary of the house, dutifully doing as Blake had asked her to.

"I died because of him," Anais spat the words venomously before composing herself. Her face became a mask of bored disinterest once more. "And you will die because of me."

Blake had heard enough—the threat to Emma's life was the final straw. Before anyone could say or do anything else, he pulled his weapon from the ether, took a step towards Anais, and slashed the blade downwards through her spectre.

All was still for a moment, as though the whole world held its breath, and then an explosion of black particles blew outwards from Anais's core. They hung in the air for a brief moment before fading into nothing. As they dissipated, Blake watched Anais's life play through in his mind's eye. She'd been abused as a child and had run away from home at a young age. Her first kill had been an accident, but a fortuitous one in that she'd taken out a criminal's rival. Her reward had been a warm bed, food to eat, and clothes to wear. From then on she'd played the role of a cold-hearted assassin. One day she'd overheard a conversation in which she'd been described as nothing more than a butcher. Later on that day all involved were found slaughtered, their bodies butchered to the point of being almost unrecognisable. Wanting to leave a calling card, Anais had placed a small piece of coloured bone in each of their left cheeks. And so it began. She never knew why the police started referring to her as Anais Bechard, she never did find out how they'd known she'd once been described as a butcher, but she took the name as her own anyway. It suited her more than Giselle Lebeau anyway.

While Blake was distracted, Anais clutched her stomach, seemingly in pain. Her face was contorted in agony, but then she burst out laughing.

"You think I needed my soul. It never did me any good in life; I don't need it in death either." She laughed so hard that she fell to her knees, whereupon she pushed her hands into the moss that had invaded Emma's lawn. A groaning sound ripped through the air, and the earth shuddered beneath Blake's feet.

"Blake!" Emma called from the sanctuary of the house, fear threading its way through her body. "Be careful!"

"Stay there," Blake barked in reply, confident that he had nothing to fear.

Blake remained standing, scythe in hand. And Anais remained on her knees, concentrating on the ground beneath her hands. It continued to heave and quake in response to whatever it was that she was doing. How was it possible? Remnants did not possess such powers. Blake knew that they could control the elements, but this? He'd never seen anything like this before. A furrow opened up in front of him, ripping the turf apart. And from the gaping jaws of the earth, a tree root emerged. It pulled itself free from the soil, spraying dirt in all directions, before rising up to stand tall in the air, with only its tip bent over. It swayed from side to side, like the cobras of Marrakech that danced to the tune of their pipe players, before darting forwards and piercing Blake's shoulder. He had no time to react; the pain that shot through his body was beyond anything he'd ever imagined possible. Yes, he'd borne witness to all kinds of physical torment through the years, but nothing had prepared him for what it actually felt like to have his own flesh torn apart. Sweat beaded on his forehead and blood seeped from the wound as the tree root jerked backwards, pulling with it sinew and muscle. Blake's legs simply gave way and he fell to the ground with a thump.

Three things happened simultaneously.

Anais laughed harder. "I thought it was going to be fun when I eventually got her, but you!" She pounded the ground with her fists, gasping for breath, caught up in the delightful incredulity of the situation.

Seith darted from where he'd been sitting and launched himself at Anais, only to pass harmlessly through her spectral being.

And Emma flew from the safety of the house to be by Blake's side. She was on the ground beside him in a fraction of a second, brushing wayward strands of hair from his face. "Blake? Blake, don't you dare leave me. You're the Keeper of Souls, for crying out loud. You're supposed to be immortal! Don't leave me."

"You should be inside," he muttered in response, his words slurred.

"Blake, look at me," Emma demanded. And Blake found himself compelled to obey. He hadn't even realised that he'd closed his eyes, but with some effort, he was able to open them. He gazed adoringly into Emma's faces, all three of them. She was all he'd ever wanted, but he hadn't known that. He'd lived his life wanting everything and more. Until he'd met her. As more blood seeped from the gaping hole in his shoulder, his life along with it, he finally realised what it meant to truly be alive.

Chapter 23 – Emma

Tuesday 23rd April 2019

Don't leave me. Don't leave me. Don't leave me. The words were stuck on repeat, playing over and over again in my mind.

My world had shrunk to what was in my immediate eyeline. Blake. Blake was wounded. Blake was dying. Blake had a huge gaping hole in his shoulder that was oozing blood. How was that even possible? Surely it wasn't, surely he'd heal? He had to, right? He was the Keeper of Souls after all. The world needed him. What would happen if he didn't exist? How would people's souls be claimed for reuse. And when had I accepted that what Blake did was necessary? My mind was a confused mess.

Leave me. Leave me. Leave me. Somewhere along the way, the loop that was playing silently for only me to hear had lost the word 'don't.' I listened to it for hours before realising that that was it—that was the answer. Blake needed to get out of my bubble.

I looked around me. Clearly hours hadn't passed. Anais was still knelt on the ground laughing. Seith crouched behind her, his maw pulled back into a silent snarl. And Ellie was hovering behind me.

"Blake," I whispered, my voice hoarse, "you need to go. Leave me, get away from me."

"Mmm-hmmm." Blake's incoherent response was mostly noncommittal.

Think, Emma, think! I commanded myself, silently willing a lightbulb moment to occur, praying harder than I'd ever prayed before, which didn't require that much effort because I'd never prayed for anything in my life, what with being a non-believer. Illumination took days but eventually an idea formed. If I could pull Blake to me from wherever he was, surely I could push him away from me to somewhere else, anywhere else.

"Blake, go away," I said.

"Nnargh."

I stood before trying again. Somewhere, miles away from where I was, I heard Ellie asking if I was okay, if she could do anything, but I couldn't afford to be distracted right now. Instead, I focussed on what I wanted, what I desired more than anything else in the world, for Blake to be somewhere else, to be anywhere else. I pictured a beach, white golden sands leading down to crystal clear blue waters that darkened further out to sea into a bright cobalt colour. The whole coastal area was empty, devoid of life, and the waves lapped gently on the shore. The sun shone brightly overhead, but there was a gentle breeze that made the air feel deliciously cool. It was exactly where I would want to be if I needed to recuperate; it was peaceful and quiet. I didn't even know if it was a real place, but I held the image firmly in my mind before saying again, "Blake. GO. AWAY."

He disappeared in an instant. Where he went, I assumed I'd never find out. I assumed Anais fully intended to end my life, and it very much seemed as though no one could stop her. Blake had removed her soul, but somehow she still had power. Seith had tried and failed. What could either Ellie or I possibly do?

Anais stopped laughing the instant that Blake vanished. "Where did he go?" she snapped, rising to her feet. Behind her, Seith's tail wagged from side to side but not in a hey-wanna-be-friends kind of way. I could almost feel the air around me reverberate from his growls as he stalked his prey, trying to work out how to end her death.

"I don't know," I answered honestly, too overwhelmed to even think about lying.

"You . . . you'll pay for that!" With a flick of her wrist, Anais sent a mini tornado gust of wind in my direction, but Ellie jumped in front of me and somehow diverted it so that all I felt was the barest breath of wind. She glanced at me and shrugged, her eyes glowing a bright electric blue. Usually her eyes were an icy cool colour, but now they were radioactive.

"How did you . . .?" Anais asked, directing her question at Ellie.

"Wouldn't you like to know?" Ellie answered, not giving anything away, not even to me. And I too wanted to know! Apparently Abaddon had gifted Ellie with more than we knew.

"I don't mind killing the both of you, you know?" Anais snarled, jabbing a finger in mine and Ellie's direction before clenching her hands, balling them into fists, ready to strike once more.

"Wait!" I called, desperate to keep her talking because I had no idea how we were getting out of this alive and I needed time to think, to come up with a plan. "How *are* you doing this? I thought remnants helped plants grow; I thought they were a cool breeze on a hot day, a spark, or a droplet of rain. You . . . you're . . . I don't know what you are."

I was surprised when Anais answered. I hadn't expected her to. "Oh, oh, this is delicious," she gloated, a smirk on her face. Her posture relaxed, her shoulders dropped and she let her arms go limp once more. She was clearly getting ready to tell us a tale, but I highly doubted it was going to be one that I liked. "It was you that gave me the idea actually, daaarling. Do you remember your night at the hospital, courtesy of little ole me?" Anais patted her chest and leaned forwards, giggling like a school child meeting her first crush.

How could I forget? I thought, but kept silent, merely encouraging her to continue with a brief nod of my head.

"Do you remember saying that you were famished?"

I pulled a face. I couldn't remember saying anything of the sort. And if Anais had been on the ward with me, wouldn't I have seen her?

"No?" Anais interrupted my idle musing. "Don't bother answering. I can tell that you don't remember. You're making a funny face. A bit like this . . ." She trailed off and grimaced. "I wouldn't do that too often if I were you; you'll give yourself worry lines."

"Hey!" I interjected, unable to keep quiet any longer, earning myself a jab in the ribs from Ellie.

"What?" Anais asked innocently. "Well, you did. And I thought—"

"You weren't on the ward that night." It was my turn to interrupt.

"Yes, I was. You see, the great thing about being dead is that you can go just about anywhere you want, which means you can hide just about anywhere too. I followed you, and I saw him watching over you. I was just too tired after my stunt with the water to do anything about the fact that you were defenceless. I was too . . . famished." Anais chose her word carefully.

A horribly distressing, uncomfortable idea started to build into a knot at the back of my mind. I had an idea where this was going, but no, surely not. Surely not. It was sickening. If I was right.

"And then your little friend came to visit. What was her name now?" Anais shifted her weight, placing her right hand on her hip and lifting her left to tap her forefinger against the side of her cheek. She looked up towards the heavens in an exaggerated display of confusion, as though she really couldn't remember my 'little friend's' name.

My stomach churned with anxiety, but I was rooted to the spot, bound in place by unseen chains that anchored my feet to the floor. *No, no, please no.* I couldn't bring myself to say anything, but Ellie found her voice. "Oh stop it with the over-acting. We all know you're better than that otherwise the police would have caught up with you."

"Fine." Anais sighed. "I ate Jennifer." Her words were said so blandly, with so little emotion, that she could have almost said anything: Fine, I ate the strawberries. Fine, I ate the chocolate. Fine, I ate the garlic. But no, she'd actually said the thing that I'd been dreading: Fine, I ate Jennifer.

My body reacted as though I'd been thumped in the stomach with a bowling ball; I turned away from Ellie and threw up on the grass next to me. The acid from my stomach burned my throat and fresh tears fell from my eyes. Poor Jennifer. Poor, sweet, messed-up Jennifer. Her life had been bad enough, but for this to happen in her death . . . . It just didn't bear thinking about.

"It's okay, I've got you," Ellie muttered quietly to me as I sank into a half crouch. She never took her eyes off Anais, but she rubbed my back slowly, giving me support and comfort. Ellie hadn't met Jennifer, but I'd told her everything about her. And even if I hadn't, she would still have stood beside me offering me her strength. Ellie was a force for good. She'd been blessed by the angels, she'd been gifted powers by them, their blood ran in her veins. With her by my side, I could get through anything. We would find a way to defeat Anais. She was after all only a remnant. A powerful one, but I shared a soul with the Keeper of Souls, and I was pissed. Ellie was kind and compassionate, but I was full of rage. The sorrow and heartache that had consumed me only moments before were replaced with anger. Much like when Grammy had died, I wrapped it around me like a shawl, drawing deeply on the comfort it offered me.

Slowly, I stood to face my foe, wiping my nose with the back of my hand. I was well aware that I looked a mess. Snot smeared my cheek, smudging the tear tracks that had dried there. My eyes were undoubtedly rimmed red, and my hair was likely a tangled knot. Without looking, I knew that I had dirt on my jeans and most likely on my T-shirt too. But those things didn't matter.

"I don't believe you," I said. "Prove it."

"Not just Jennifer, by the way," Anais continued conversationally, as though she hadn't heard me. "The buzz from her made me want more. I doubt you'll find a living remnant in the whole of Blackpool."

"Prove. It."

"Surely the fact that I am here is proof enough? You saw your beloved take my soul, didn't you? Yet here I stand, able to do what I shouldn't be able to do, able to fight the compulsion that would otherwise keep me in one place."

"That only proves that you've done something. I want proof that you murdered Jennifer."

"I didn't murder her," Anais scoffed. "She was already dead. I just ate her."

"Semantics. Now. Prove. It."

"Fine," Anais muttered, rolling her eyes before blurring slightly and transforming into Jennifer.

I gasped aloud. For all intents and purposes, Jennifer, and not Anais, now stood in front of me. She looked exactly as she had when I'd met her at the hospital, drowning in that damn hoodie with scuffed shoes on her feet. Her heart-shaped face looked even more haunted than before, though, her dark brown eyes were brimming with unshed tears and her skin had taken on a ghastly pallor.

Without thinking, I took a step forwards, only for Ellie to grab my arm and pull me back. "That proves nothing," she said, "only that you know what Jennifer looks like."

"Oh for God's sake." Anais may have looked like Jennifer, but her attitude and her mannerisms were still very much her own.

"Well?"

"I don't know why I haven't just killed you already, but okay. What was it Jennifer told you? When she whispered in your ear? Do you remember?"

I nodded. Of course I remembered. Jennifer had told me I was the Key and that I could control Blake. Neither pieces of information had been news. I knew I could reach out and pull Blake to me when I wanted him. And being the Key . . . well, that was getting old now. So what if Blake and I shared a soul? It didn't mean I could do any of the things that he could do. I couldn't sense death in others or reap people's souls or witness each life lost. I couldn't go wherever I wanted, whenever I wanted. All I could do was make Blake come to me. Or was that all I could do? I had just made him leave after all. And once upon a time, a lifetime ago, I'd wondered if I could compel him to do more, but I'd never experimented, nor even followed the stray thought any further down the rabbit hole to see how far it went. I'd never wanted to feel like I was forcing Blake to do anything against his will. But maybe now I would have to? Maybe Anais had given me the answer. Even if Blake didn't know how to exorcise a remnant, was it that easy? Could I simply order him to do it? Of course, to do that, I needed him to be alive and able.

"I see that you do remember," Anais continued. "Do I need to remind you, or do you believe me now?"

"Tell me what she said," I demanded, stalling for time. While I had the beginnings of a plan, it wasn't a very well thought out one. If only I could freeze time and discuss the details with Ellie and Blake. Why was that not one of Ellie's abilities?

Anais chuckled, a deep husky-sounding laugh. She was enjoying every minute of this, every second of my suffering brought her immense pleasure. She was truly evil. "Do the words, 'you are the Key' mean anything to you? And what about, 'you can control everything he does'?" She paused briefly, waiting for her words to sink in. "Oh good! They do resonate with you." My face must have given her the only reply she needed.

Anais may as well have driven a spike through my heart with her words. All along I'd known she was telling the truth but having her confirm it made it so very real. She'd actually done it; she'd consumed another living being for her own benefit. Well, Jennifer hadn't been living exactly, but she had been sentient, capable of thought and emotion. A sharp pain bloomed in my chest, radiating outwards, easing into a dull ache as it spread outwards. I fell to the ground again, collapsing under the weight of everything. Panic threatened to engulf me, my chest felt tight. It felt like a boa constrictor had coiled itself around me and was slowly crushing me. Not that I'd ever had that happen to know what it would feel like of course.

Ellie crouched beside me again, wrapping her arms around my shoulders. "Emma," she said, her words quiet, for my benefit only. "We need to get out of here, back to the house where we'll be safe. We need time; we need to come up with a new plan."

A new plan . . . . I'd had the beginnings of a new plan . . . . Ellie's words helped to snap me out of my panic attack.

"I've got one, Ellie. I just need to talk to Blake."

"Blake? Isn't he . . ."

"No, I don't think so. Can you keep her distracted for a few minutes?" I glanced up at Anais, who'd taken herself off on a little walk around my garden. She was showing off, using her ghastly gifts to cause more damage in my once perfect garden. She'd spun up a mini tornado and was slowly ripping apart my shrubs while the earth in my flowerbeds was being dug into by unseen hands. And I thought Cooper had made a mess when he'd dug himself a little bed in among the plants! Despite saying that she was going to end both me and Ellie, she didn't seem all that interested in actually doing it. I was starting to think that what she really enjoyed was the game. She loved causing distress in others. If we were dead, our suffering would end. And she'd have no one else to play with.

"Erm, sure. Leave it with me." Ellie sounded dubious, but she did stand and take a step towards Anais. "Hey! Leave the garden alone."

I didn't hear Anais's reply. Instead, I remained on the ground and continued to play the grief-stricken victim, my hands covering my face, my fingers splayed so that I could watch Anais covertly. Actually, though, my mind had cleared. I felt confident, but for my plan to work, I needed Blake. I needed to be able to control him (which I didn't feel good about, but given the circumstances, I assumed he'd be okay with it), and I needed him to be able to see through my eyes, something he'd only ever done once before.

Blake! I shouted in my mind. *Blake! Can you hear me?* I had no idea where I'd sent him and no idea where he was now, which wasn't the greatest starting position in the world. While Blake could feel my pull regardless of where he was, to hear me, he had to be relatively nearby. *If you can hear me, whatever you do, don't come here.*

Stop shouting, my head hurts.

Does it really? I'd assumed that as soon as Blake was outside of my bubble, he would have reformed, completely healed.

Why would I lie? Blake had obviously abandoned all reason in favour of diving happily into his own personal despair. I was starting to suspect that what he was feeling was only the memory of what he'd experienced.

Pfft! Your head doesn't hurt. You're an incorporeal being, remember? I need you to deal with Anais.

There was a moment of silence before Blake responded. *She can't be stopped. She attacked me. My shoulder, I can still feel where the tree root pierced my skin. White-hot pokers would have caused less pain.*

Blake, snap out of it, I commanded. Now was not the time for Blake to have a crisis of faith.

She's too powerful, Blake moaned. *You need to get out of there, get back into the house where you'll be safe.* Oh good, at least he was thinking about me while wallowing in his own misery, and he was wallowing in misery. Now that I'd re-established our connection, his emotions were swamping my own. His confidence had been shattered; he'd been arrogant when he'd faced Anais, sure that he could best her. But he hadn't. Not only that, not only had he failed to eliminate her as a threat, but she'd fought back and harmed him. Nothing had ever caused Blake to feel anything before, let alone pain, and he was not coping very well with his first real negative experience of life.

Blake, stop this right now. Without knowing exactly what to do or how to compel Blake, I visualised a storm. Black clouds darkened the sky, thunder rumbled, and lightning flickered. And then the clouds started to clear: first they lightened, slowly turning white, before drifting lazily out of sight leaving behind clear blue skies. The thunder quietened, and the lightning ceased.

Blake stilled. *Don't do that. I've told you before, I am not your puppet.*

I'm sorry, Blake, I really am, but I need you right now.

You have my attention. Blake was pissed, with a capital P. He really didn't like the fact that he was at my mercy. And now I knew that I could make him do anything I wanted, even if he didn't know how to do what I commanded, he could make it happen. That's what Abaddon had been warning Ellie about, that's why I was so dangerous as the Key. Maybe Joanne's instinct was the right one, maybe Ellie should act against me. But that was tomorrow's problem, first of all we all had to survive the day.

Anais is so powerful because she's been consuming other remnants. Jennifer, Blake. She ate Jennifer. My stomach felt queasy saying the words. *But you can do something about it. You can force a remnant from this plane. You can end her.*

That's not true.

It is. Jennifer told me. Remember what she said at the hospital? She said she avoided you because you could make her leave.

That doesn't mean I can perform an exorcism.

You can, Blake, and if you don't know how, I can make you. I felt Blake's wrath rising, but I rushed on, needing him to hear the rest of my plan before he exploded in fury. *You can see through my eyes, can't you?* Blake didn't acknowledge me to be right, but I knew I was. *Well, you'll stay hidden in the house . . .*

I am in the house already.

. . . and I'll compel you to get rid of Anais. It'll be easy because she won't be expecting it. We'll catch her off guard because she knows you're the only one who can actually do anything to her, but she won't see you. Even Seith seems unable to act; he passed right through her when he attacked.

I don't agree.

Blake. . . honey. . . my life's in danger. Ellie's life's in danger. And unless you can come up with another plan, we haven't got time for you to learn how to do what needs to be done.

Blake paused before reluctantly agreeing. *Fine, but only because your life is in danger. You will never compel me ever again.*

I promise I won't. I don't want to do it even now. I wish there was another way, but . . .

But there isn't.

Not that I can think of, no. I paused, giving Blake a minute to get used to the idea, but we didn't really have all that much time. Anais was bound to lose interest in toying with us sometime soon. We had to act. *Blake, how do I allow you to see through my eyes?*

Concentrate on your vision. Really see the world around you. Think about every blade of grass, every leaf, every flower. Lose yourself in your senses.

Before standing, I scanned my ruined garden quickly, concentrating on every single thing that I could see. Seith still lurked at the far end of the garden. He was crouched on his haunches, ready to strike, but there was nothing for him to attack. Anais was not like Peter; she was already dead. There was no flesh and bone for Seith to sink his teeth into. Seith couldn't help us today.

Anais herself was standing with Ellie. If I didn't know any better, the two of them could have been socialising at a family barbecue. Anais was laughing at something that Ellie had said, but Ellie only scowled back at her. Ellie was a sight to behold, she glowed a bright white colour, and her eyes shone an electric blue. Clearly the angel blood that ran in her veins was active.

"Anais Bechard!" I stood and turned my body so that I was facing the ghoul in my garden. It was time. "Or should I say Giselle Lebeau!"

"Oh, you're back with us, are you? This one's been making me laugh. She keeps saying you're going to send me straight to hell." She waved her hand briefly at Ellie. "I'm having so much fun making your lives a misery, I've decided to let you live for a while longer. You'll both be at my mercy every single day of your lives, never knowing what I'm going to do next or when I'm going to do it."

"I am going to send you to hell." I squared my shoulders and shuffled my feet so that I was standing in a braced fighting position. "You've no right to do the things you've done. It's over."

Now, Blake! I barked at him, *Exorcise the bitch, exorcise Anais.* With everything I had, I compelled Blake to do as I asked, repeating my command over and over again, using Anais's real name, hoping it would make my 'spell' more powerful. *Exorcise Giselle Lebeau, exorcise Giselle Lebeau, exorcise Giselle Lebeau . . . .*

Without knowing how or why, I began chanting in a language that I'd never heard, all the while reciting the same phrase on a loop in the silence of my mind: *Exorcise Giselle Lebeau!* Blake wasn't just using my eyes to witness his first banishment, he was using my body to perform the act.

Anais laughed at first; my plan was working. Her arrogance was her undoing. She was so confident that there was nothing I could do to her that she didn't even fight what was happening. I saw the exact moment when she realised she'd been wrong. She stilled, and doubt flickered across her face. Her forehead creased into a slight frown; her eyes lost their sparkle. She clutched at her chest. Her body seemed to expand, before contracting in on itself. It rose up off the ground, all the while pulsing and shimmering, eventually losing all of its definition until it was nothing more than a humanoid shape suspended in mid-air. And then it fractured, breaking into five or six discrete pieces, each of which exploded outwards. It was a fireworks display to end all fireworks displays.

Anais's scream could be heard until every single particle of her being had drifted away, but I didn't hear because in the moment that Anais's body had shattered into a million pieces, Blake took my hand. He looked at me, I looked at him, and then we smiled at each other. It was over.

Chapter 24 – Emma

Saturday 4ᵗʰ May 2019

"Are you sure you want to do this, Emma?" Ellie asked, not for the first time.

"Yes, absolutely, one hundred percent."

"He'll think you're crazy."

"I don't care. Jennifer would want me to do it."

"You don't know that for a fact."

"I don't need to know it for a fact. I know it in my heart. She wanted her mum to find some peace. We obviously can't go and see her, but her husband can, if they're still married, of course."

Ellie and I were walking arm-in-arm down a residential street in the centre of Blackpool. Terraced houses lined both sides of the road, flanking it like sentinels guarding their residents. Parked cars cluttered what little space there was between the two rows of dwellings, sometimes half-on and half-off the pavement, other times wholly off it, and more than once all the way on it! As a consequence, we had to weave our way through the various obstacles as we searched for the right house.

We were looking for number 342, which was where Jennifer had been brought up. It was also where Jennifer's mum had suffocated her before slitting her own wrists. It was a miracle that the woman had survived really.

"I've found it."

Ellie glanced in the direction that I was looking and laughed out loud. "Yes, I've found it too." Blake was standing on the apex of the roof of one of the houses, maybe ten or twelve up the road from where we were walking. He was dressed in his preferred attire, his fitted black jacket, a black shirt, black trousers, and, of course, black knee-length boots. He only ever changed his look when we were mixing with other people. He'd already scoped out the house and had been able to confirm that Jennifer's dad still lived there.

"It's so weird that you can see him all of the time now," I commented. "Have you seen anything else?"

"No. Although I haven't really looked since I tried to *see* Seith. Abaddon explained that her gift of sight will let me see the truth in everyone and I just need to let it happen. I'm assuming she means angels and demons, but I'm not sure if I'm ready for that."

"Hmmm, no. I can understand that. I wonder how many demons there are on Earth."

"I got the impression that there are enough of them that if I go looking, I'd find one."

"Nice. What are we going to do about all of that?"

"I don't know." Ellie sighed. "Mum still says that we may have to . . . well, you know."

I laughed, knowing full well what she meant and why she didn't want to say it out loud. Who would have thought that I'd be okay talking about the fact that Joanne wanted me dead? Well, that wasn't exactly the truth. I'd now accepted that Joanne loved me as she always had. She just subscribed to the many-lives-outweigh-the-one theory. It wasn't that she wanted anything to happen to me, but if it was my life or the end of the world.... Occasionally I wondered how she'd feel if it was Ellie's life or the end of the world, but I guess we'd never know the answer to that. Ellie had forgiven her, and the two were slowly repairing their relationship, but I was still avoiding her. I'd now survived more than one attempt on my life; I intended on keeping it.

Jennifer's childhood home was a tiny terraced house. It was built from traditional red brick and had dark wooden windows—two on the upper floor looking down onto the street and one on the lower floor next to the front door. It was set back from the road, courtesy of an even smaller front yard that was enclosed by a low brick wall. I pushed open the gate fully expecting it to squeak loudly, but it didn't. The house was small, but it appeared to have been well cared for. On either side of the dark blue front door were two pots, both planted with miniature evergreens. As a gardener, I tended not to plant them because they always outgrew their pots, but they looked smart beside the doorway.

Ellie reached the front door just before me. She stretched and knocked before stepping back to stand next to me. She hadn't quite gotten used to the new strength that Abaddon had gifted her with, and as a consequence, she hammered quite loudly.

"Blimey, Ellie, are you trying to raise the dead?" I joked, only to be glared at in response. She may have been planning to tell me off in the way that only she could, but before she could answer, Jennifer's dad opened the door, letting me off the hook.

"Hello, Mr. Jones," I smiled warmly. "I'm sorry to bother you. My name's Emma Moore, and this is Ellie Chapman-Bell." I indicated Ellie. "We were friends with Jennifer."

"Jennifer?" Mr. Jones gasped. "But she's been . . . she left us . . . that is . . . she died some time ago."

"I know she did. I'm aware of what happened. Listen, would you mind if we came in? I promise we're not crackpots."

I don't know what was going through Mr. Jones' head, but he stood to one side. "The lounge is through there."

"Thanks so much," I answered, brushing past him as I stepped where he indicated.

"Tea?" Mr. Jones asked when he eventually joined me and Ellie after closing up at the front.

"That would be nice," Ellie replied. "Do you want me to get it? You must be confused by our visit."

"Erm, sure, whatever." Mr. Jones couldn't have been much older than my parents, but he looked ancient and seemed uncertain about everything. He settled into a chair by the window while I perched on the sofa and Ellie busied herself in the kitchen. For the moment, I kept still and studied him quietly. He was neither tall nor short, fat nor thin. Instead he was lean but soft. He sat hunched over in his chair, his head hung low. He had a shock of greying hair on his head and wore thick-rimmed glasses that did nothing to hide the dark shadows underneath his eyes. But he was smartly dressed in a blue plaid shirt, grey corduroy trousers, and a woollen cardigan that was buttoned up the middle.

We passed two or three minutes in silence until Ellie came bustling in with a tray laden with mugs of steaming tea and a plate filled with what looked like digestives. Or perhaps they were hobnobs.

"I hope you don't mind, Mr. Jones, but I raided your biscuit tin." She smiled while handing a brew to each of us before joining me on the sofa.

"Please, love, call me Richard. No one calls me Mr. Jones anymore."

"Richard it is then," I answered before sipping my tea, wondering how the hell I was going to explain that I'd only actually met Jennifer after she'd died. "So, here's the thing," I started, "you're probably not going to believe me, but well, the thing is . . . I, erm, I can . . ."

"Stop rambling, Emma," Ellie chided. "Mr. Jones, Richard, this will sound completely insane, but I promise you it's true. Emma can see the dead, and she recently met your daughter, Jennifer."

I watched as the blood drained from Richard's face. He turned ashen in front of my eyes. "But that's not possible, is it? How is it possible?"

"It's a bit of a long story," Ellie remarked, her eyebrows raised.

"So . . . the thing is, I'm soulmates with the Grim Reaper . . ."

Keeper of Souls, Blake corrected from somewhere overhead.

No one's heard of the Keeper of Souls, Blake. For today, you're the Grim Reaper.

Hmph.

"And as a consequence, I can see ghosts."

Remnants.

Yes, Blake. I know.

"No one can see ghosts, it's not . . ."

"I know what you're thinking, Richard, but I can promise you that I met with Jennifer. She was a beautiful young woman." I went on to describe what she looked like and what she'd been wearing every time I'd seen her.

"Huh." Richard shook his head in disbelief. "She loved that bloody sweatshirt, only ever took it off when her mum made her because it needed a wash." His face fell when he referred to his wife.

"How is Jennifer's mum, Richard? How's she doing?"

"She's locked in the nuthouse. How do you think she's doing?"

"That's why we came, actually. Jennifer doesn't blame her mum, or you for what happened. She wanted you both to be at peace."

"How could she not blame her mum? Or me? Her mum literally suffocated her. Kids nowadays are always complaining that their parents are suffocating them, but they don't know what they're saying. My Jennifer was murdered. And I did nothing to stop it. I knew her mum was ill, but I just never expected it. Not that."

"Oh Richard." My heart shattered into a million pieces. The pain and guilt that he was carrying around was almost palpable in the air. I set my tea on the floor, slid from the sofa, and hugged him around the knees. "Jennifer doesn't blame either of you. She knew her mum was unwell and that you did everything you could. When I met her at the Vic, she was happy; she was content where she was. She travelled with her mum to the hospital and stayed there until she knew that her life had been saved. She's been there ever since."

"She has? Could I . . . could you talk to her for me?"

Damn! I'd been hoping this wouldn't come up. In fact, this was the one part of Jennifer's story that I'd been hoping to gloss over. I hugged Richard tight before moving back to the sofa. "I'd love to, but I'm afraid I can't. She's gone now. She was ready. Ghosts tend to move on when they've done what they stayed here to do, and Jennifer had done what she needed to do. She'd told me that she didn't blame you so that I could pass on the message." It was a good enough explanation, one that I was hoping would satisfy him.

"She's gone? My little girl is at peace?"

"Yes, Richard, she's gone and she's at peace. I was hoping that you could talk to her mum and make sure she knows that Jennifer doesn't blame her for what she did."

"Well, I'll talk to her, but I can't promise she'll listen."

"Is it that bad?" Ellie asked.

"Yes. She lives mostly in her own little world now."

"Well, if you could try, that would be great," I answered, smiling encouragingly at Richard. He looked different from when we'd first knocked on the door. Colour was returning to his cheeks, and there was a sparkle in his eyes that hadn't been there before. At least Ellie and I had done one good thing, even if we couldn't help Jennifer's mum.

"I'll try," Richard answered before suddenly laughing out loud. "Girls!" he exclaimed. "I feel like a weight has been lifted from my shoulders. This calls for something more than a cup of tea in celebration." He reached inside his cardigan and pulled a hip flask from a pocket that was hidden in the depths of his clothing. God knows why they were called hip flasks when he'd had it stashed in a chest-height pocket. He took a swig of whatever it was that was contained within the flask before offering it to both me and Ellie.

"No, thank you." We both shook our heads, and the flask disappeared back inside of his clothing.

"Richard, we should get going; I'm sure you've got a lot of things to think about," I said. Ellie nodded in agreement and jumped to her feet. She started clearing away, but Richard stopped her.

"No, don't, love. Leave it, I'll do it when you've gone." He pulled her into an embrace, having stood up when she did. "Thank you so much, thank you."

I too rose and was enveloped in one of Richard's hugs. There was nothing romantic in it, he was just a lonely old man who'd had the weight of the world lifted from his shoulders. "Thank you for finding me, for telling me what you did. I don't know what to say; I'm so grateful. I'll never be able to repay you."

"You've nothing to repay, Richard. Jennifer helped me, and now I've helped you."

"You most certainly have, my dear. I think I'll sleep properly tonight for the first time in many years."

"Good! Start living your life again, Richard. Jennifer would want you to." As we'd been talking, Richard had guided me and Ellie to the front door. I reached for the handle, twisted it, and stepped out into the sunshine. The clouds parted and a beam of light shone down onto me. I'd been blessed from above, but for how long?

Epilogue

Sunday 5th May 2019

"Well? Has the haunting ceased?"

"It seems to have done. She's moving about freely again, and nothing untoward happens to her now."

"No gale force winds?"

"No, nothing. No gale force winds, no fires, and certainly no 'gas leaks.'"

"Charlotte really believes it was a gas leak?"

"She does. No one can come up with any other explanation. She's persuaded herself that that's what it was."

"People are fools."

"I'm a person."

"Yes, you are. And the cleansing? The police, have they found anything?"

"They didn't even test the blood. They assumed it was animal."

"Good, good. It will really start to take effect now that the haunting has ceased. We need the Key to be purified before we can act. She's back at work, I take it?"

"She is. She's been back for a week now."

"Okay. Keep an eye on her. I'll let you know what to do next and when. You're dismissed."

The End . . . well, not quite yet!

A FINAL WORD FROM THE AUTHOR

If you enjoyed *A Grim Haunt*, why don't you follow me on Instagram? I use Instagram to share my life as an author and to post updates about forthcoming events / publications.

I'd also ask that you take 5-10 minutes to leave me a review on your preferred platform. Reviews will not only help me to build my credibility, they'll also encourage other readers to pick up my work. You don't need to write *War and Peace*; a simple 'I liked it' will do. Thank you in advance.

My Instagram handle is: rachel21stanley